A FADED SIGHT

ANUJ GAUTAM

I want to dedicate this book to my family and friends for their belief in my work. Without God's grace, none of this would be possible, so I am grateful for the different opportunities to showcase my work to the world.

Contents

Acknowledgements

I want to express my deepest gratitude to my friends and family, who supported me throughout the writing of this book. Special thanks to my brother, Abhishek, and sister-in-law, Shruti, who edited this book. Also, special thanks to my friend Kritika, whose exceptional design skills helped me create a cover for the book. I am also grateful to the Notion Press team for their publishing platform, expertise, and dedication. Finally, to the readers – your support means everything.

Prologue

The night of graduation was supposed to be a celebration. Laughter, joy, and endless promises of the future filled the air. But for Ella, something pivoted; she vanished into the shadows, leaving behind nothing but gossip and chaos. No one could explain where she went or why. For Dave, the disappearance shattered his world. Ella wasn't just another friend; she was a part of his life. The mystery of her absence clung to him for a long time. Then, one afternoon, while passing through a crowded street, Dave saw her—or at least he thought he did. From that moment, Dave knew he couldn't let it go. He had to find her, to uncover the truth, no matter the cost. But as he delved deeper into her disappearance, the path became twisted, leading him to places he never imagined. One thing was clear: both their stories are intertwined and unfinished.

I

A Silent Storm

It was a beautiful sunny day in Pinewood Town because of the spring season; the trees were full of majestic flowers of different colours—the birds were chirping, which was more of a melody for the local people of the small place in the North of the country.

Dave, an aspiring artist of 25, was asleep in his room. He was averagely built, had long dark hair, pointed facial features and a pale skin tone, and was lost in the imagination of his next great art. However, his sleep and peace of mind were disrupted when he received a call.

"Who is it?" Dave cried, still half asleep. "What?" His sleep vanished within a second. At that moment, his life was about to change, and it was only the beginning.

Dave was studying art at Pinewood University. He was from Ivory Town, about 100 miles from his current location. His family consisted of his father, mother, and brother, Gil, who was still in school. Dave's parents owned a small hotel in their hometown; business-wise, things were going well for them.

However, on the other side of the town, things took a drastic turn for Dave. He received a call from Elliot, one of Dave's closest friends, who broke the news of their missing friend, Ella.

Dave hurriedly got ready and was on his way to meet his friend. He took a cab to Elliot's place—the guy was a local student at the same university but was pursuing journalism in another department. He reached the home and was welcomed by Elliot, who was eagerly waiting for his buddy.

"What happened?" Dave immediately asked his friend.

"Just come in," Elliot asked Dave to come inside and made him sit on the couch. Elliot was of medium height, had fair skin, a round face with rectangular spectacles, and curly hair with toned muscles. His parents, Mr and Mrs Grant, were not home then. They both worked at the local press, so it is evident that Elliot knew about the case before anyone else.

"Ella, she's gone. Everyone is looking for her." Elliot was freaked out by the entire situation.

"You already told me that on the phone. But what happened?" Dave had only one question on his mind.

"Well, when was the last time you saw her?" Elliot asked eagerly.

"Ummm." Dave thought for a bit. "Maybe last Friday, after her graduation ceremony at the college. But why does it matter?"

"Well, her parents Mr and Mrs Cooper filed the missing complaint yesterday, in the evening."

"Yes, I saw her the last time at her house when we all came back from celebrating. Today is Sunday. Are they sure that she's not with one of her friends?"

"They tried to reach her but her phone was switched off. Plus it wouldn't matter as Ella's phone was found in her room. And after calling her entire friend circle, the Cooper family decided to go to the police."

"Hmmm, they didn't contact me." Dave was confused.

Elliot was pissed a little. "Like, it could've made a difference?"

"You're right. We should check on them." The man nodded with tension.

Both friends left for Ella's house, which was on the North end of the town. The streets were buzzing with the crowd as it was already approaching afternoon. The two friends were on a small blue scooter; it was an effective means of transport considering the tight demographic of the town.

They reached their destination within 10 minutes. Elliot parked his scooter at the front of the house's gate. However, Dave didn't wait a second for his pal. He had already entered Ella's house to find her parents in distress. Mr and Mrs Cooper were pleased to see Elliot and Dave. They had known both of them for the past few years and had met them on multiple occasions.

They were expecting a new revelation about her whereabouts. Mr Cooper was a healthy-looking middle-aged man with fair skin, round spectacles, and a somewhat edgy face. He wore a plain white shirt that he somehow managed to tuck in his pants over his broad belly.

Meanwhile, Mrs Cooper was an elegant-looking and charming woman with her tall posture, dark brown hair, round face, and big cheeks.

However, the recent tragedy had transformed her into a depressed and sad being within a few hours. Although worried, she didn't hesitate to welcome the two friends into her home.

Dave and Elliot took their places in the big room. It had a big dome-shaped opening, which was part of the design, and many fancy features, like paintings and different antiques.

"Would you like some water?" Mrs Cooper asked solemnly. She was clearly upset and on the cusp of shedding tears.

"No, Mrs Cooper, we are fine." Elliot spoke for both of them.

Mr Cooper took a seat in front of them with an upset face.

"Mr Cooper, everything will be alright." Dave tried to console the middle-aged man. At that point, Mrs Cooper stood by her husband, keeping her right hand on his left shoulder.

"I don't know what happened," the man said. She was excited to graduate from college. We had a great time on Friday. And all of a sudden, she's gone." Mr Cooper started crying as he held his sinking head by his right arm.

"Don't worry, Mr Cooper." Dave paused. "Can you tell us exactly what happened?"

Mr Cooper calmed himself, considering the situation was getting a bit awkward.

"So, it was yesterday—Ella woke up in the morning, probably set for heading out. I didn't know what was up with her? I asked her but she dismissed my question."

"Really, what did she tell you?" Dave asked without any hesitation. Meanwhile, Elliot felt a little embarrassed. He didn't anticipate Dave to be vocal and interrogatory towards Ella's family.

"Nothing, she's just wanted to get some fresh air."

"Yes, she was acting a bit hasty last morning." Mrs Cooper added. "But we both decided to let her be. Maybe she was stressed about everything. Women do feel like that sometimes."

"Yes, you're right." Dave agreed.

"However, the clock struck seven in the evening and we both were worried."

"We tried to reach on her cell phone but there was no reply. Ultimately, I found her cell in her room." Mrs Cooper said in despair.

"So, afterwards, you filed her missing complaint at the police station."

"Yes, we both went to the police department, and they are searching for her." There was silence for a moment. "Dave, do you know what was going through her mind? You guys were close." Mr Cooper asked Dave, who was speechless for a moment.

"Umm, Mr Cooper, I am sorry, but I learned about all this from Elliot. I wish I knew what Ella was up to, but unfortunately, I don't have a clue." The man dismissed any connection in an instant as if he were related to the matter.

The parents were disappointed, and who could blame them. Their only daughter was missing, and the whole of Pinewood was struck with fear and questions.

"What about you Elliot? Do you know where Ella could've gone?"

Elliot, too, didn't have anything to say about the situation. He nodded in disagreement so much that he gestured to Dave, using his elbow to leave the place. Dave wanted to stay at the Coopers, but Elliot wanted to go out.

"We should leave now," Elliot said in a remorseful tone. "I need to be somewhere," he added.

"Alright boys." Surprisingly, Mr Cooper didn't pressure them to stay.

"What, at least have some breakfast?" Mrs Cooper was looking forward to one of them being with them. However, Mr Cooper understood Elliot's whereabouts.

"We're fine, Mrs. Cooper. Thank you once again for asking." The two stood up. "If you need anything, we're here for you."

"Alright." Mr Cooper sounded as if he didn't care much about anything else.

They both left; however, Dave still felt guilty about leaving Ella's parents. He was more empathetic than Elliot, who always rushed to get in or out of a situation.

"Man, we could've stayed with them for a bit longer," Dave said confusingly. "I mean, what's the rush?"

"My bad but I'm not feeling well." Elliot came up with an indefinite excuse.

"Are you alright?" Dave enquired, who had no idea about Elliot's situation.

"Nah, I need to go back home. Rest for a while."

"But what's wrong?" The confused Dave asked again.

"I'll talk to you later. I hope you can jog home."

Elliot went to his blue scooter, put on the helmet and left Dave in front of Cooper's house. Dave was still bewildered by the situation but didn't try to intervene in Elliot's personal matters. Maybe he was traumatic. However, he was in the middle of the town with no sense of urgency.

One of his close friends was missing, while the other was having a sort of panic attack. With nowhere to go, Dave returned to spend time with Ella's parents. He knew that they both needed some kind of moral support in such a dreadful situation.

So, Dave once again knocked on the doors of the Cooper family. They were not surprised to see the young man again at their door. It was as if they had no notion about his presence a few moments ago. He got inside and calmly sat by Mr Cooper, who was on a phone call then.

"Who is it?" Dave asked Mrs Cooper, who was standing in front.

"I think it's the police."

Dave calmly waited for the phone call to be over. Mrs Cooper went inside. Her phone also rang after the thematic ringtone noise came from the room inside, down the hall.

A few minutes passed, and Dave carefully listened to the conversation between the father and the officer on the other side. It was difficult for Dave to interpret what was going on with the two. However, Mr Cooper got off the call to talk with Dave.

"Is Elliot alright? He was in a hurry?" Mr Cooper asked formally.

"He had some urgent work, but he's fine. I just wanted a breath of fresh air." Dave dismissed Elliot's sudden departure awkwardly.

"So, where'd he go?"

"To his home, I guess." Dave looked at his old watch with a withered brown strap. But who knows? He's a busy man."

"And what about you?" Mr Cooper looked at Dave with a severe gaze. "Don't you have classes today?"

Dave hesitated a bit before opening his mouth. "Mr Cooper, today is Sunday!"

"Oh God, it's just, I am a little dazed." He took a moment. "I don't know what to do? Where is my girl?" The man broke into tears while Dave was silent.

"We will find her," Dave leaned forward confidently. However, he had no idea about her friend. "So, what do the police say? Are there any updates from their end?"

"Nah, they're just investigating but I don't think they are up to something."

Dave sat for a couple of hours with Ella's family. Many calls came with only one question: 'Where is Ella?' But no one had an answer.

Dave went out multiple times to get fresh air in such a mess. He couldn't see so many tears and sadness continuously. The sun was heading towards the afternoon, and still, there was no progress on the case.

A bunch of police officers came and left Ella's place. They spoke with the family about the whole scenario. Dave also listened to what the police had to say, but to his surprise, none of them had any clue about the missing girl.

One tall officer in a black uniform approached Dave for questioning. The man had a lanky build, a pointy face, and a bit of white hair in his thick black beard. Dave was intimidated by the man's presence and was nervous before speaking to him.

"So you must be Dave?"

"Yes, officer." He replied as he stood before the officer—who sensed that the man was acting weirdly.

"So, how do you know Ella? And were you too close?"

Dave took some time before replying to the posed questions.

"Ella and I met about four years back at a college party. Both of us were juniors, and from there, our relationship—I am sorry, friendship—started."

"You are her boyfriend, right?" Police asked with curiosity.

"No, no. I have known her for a long time, but we are not in a relationship." Dave made his point very clear.

"But she was in a relationship?" Police came back to the same question.

"Not any I heard of but she was mysterious and it wouldn't surprise me if she was going out with someone."

"You too were close. Don't you know about her love life or relationships?"

"Umm, no sir, I am vague about that part of her life." Dave again dismissed any claims coming his way.

"Who told you about the missing girl?" The officer asked Dave.

"Elliot told me." He took a pause. "He's one of my friends from college."

"Would you mind if you give me his number?"

"Sure, here I'll share it right away." Dave sent Elliot's number to the officer's cell.

"Alright, thank you for your time." The police officer returned to his subordinates and left Dave after a few moments of briefing. Now, he was back to the parents, who talked to the senior officer the whole time. They all discussed the case for a bit longer, but ultimately, the officers left.

Dave, too, followed their pursuit and finally left the place as if it was the last time he'd be there.

Days, weeks and finally, several months passed, and there was no sign of Ella. The case became a huge deal in Pinewood for some time, but most people were over it except for some.

Ella's parents were still in shock, and the loss of their only daughter was something that not even time could heal. Elliot finished college and was preparing for his further examinations—he wanted to land a job in the administration.

As for Dave, he finished his art course and was ready to explore further his career by leaving Pinewood for the city. However, Ella's loss is a difficult phase in Dave's life, and he partially blames himself for the incident for not being there for her if she was struggling.

II

A Normal Life

East City was one of the closest places to small towns like Pinewood, Hilltown, and Silver Lake. This was why most people, especially students, came there to hunt for jobs or work. Dave was one of them. He graduated six months ago and was now looking for work opportunities.

It's been a year since Ella went missing, and most people have moved on from the case. Even Dave is occupied with his life, and even though he thinks about her daily, there is no point in losing his sanity over the unfortunate event.

On the other hand, he and Elliot haven't talked in so long, and maybe their friendship is almost over. It was right after the case that Elliot kept his distance from everyone. Nonetheless, Dave was too busy to think about the past as he was living with his elder cousin, Nick, the marketing head of a local startup.

Dave was looking for jobs in design and advertising, and thanks to the city's diversity, he had a couple of interviews lined up for himself. Now, he needed to show up and live up to his credentials.

Nick had a small apartment with one big hall and two small rooms. He was a couple of years older than Dave and had the physique of a trained bodybuilder. He was a disciplined man who was always dedicated to his work. He was an inspiration to Dave, who was still struggling to reach the breakfast table by being a lazy ass.

"So, you're ready for your interview tomorrow?" Nick asked the half-asleep Dave.

"Hmm." He murmured, and then he returned to the question. "Oh, yes. I am pretty confident and looking forward to tomorrow."

"What role are you applying for?" Nick took a bite from his cereal. "Is it design or art?"

"Mostly design, but that only depends on the project." Dave thought for a second. "Plus, it's a long road. First, I need to crack the interview." He looked towards his cousin. "You know what I mean."

"Yeah, right." Nick went back to enjoy his platter before remembering something. "Dave, we are out of cereal." Nick pulled out two mint bills from his pocket and handed it to Dave. "Maybe you can grab some groceries from the store below."

"Yeah, no problem." He took the money and stood up. "I'll get freshen up, and then I'll leave."

"Alright. I'll see you in the evening."

Nick finished his breakfast and left for work while Dave got ready for the small gig in his hand. He made a few calls before leaving the place—mostly work-related and one to his mother. He also had some paperwork left for tomorrow's interview, which he needed to finalise.

After leaving the place, Dave went straight to the store. He bought many items, and on his way back to the apartment, he got his paperwork set by the local stationer.

Now, he was done for the day—everything took around an hour to complete. However, Dave didn't want to spend all day in the flat.

So, he called one of his friends, Simon, who lived in East City and was also free after graduation from the same place. They both set to meet at a local cafeteria for breakfast. Dave took a cab to the place and reached before his friend; meanwhile, Simon came in his car.

Simon was a tall dude with an average build, pale skin, a round face, and curly hair. He was wearing a regular tee with black jeans. He was enrolled in the same course as Dave; however, he finished his graduation a bit later due to some examination-related complications. Nonetheless, Simon was also looking for a job, but he was a bit late on the schedule.

Both friends visited a restaurant named "Fast Life," which was more ironic considering the two were some of the most free and slow people in the city.

"How's it going?" Dave asked his friend as he stood from his seat.

"Nothing much, what's up with you." Simon sat in front of his friend. He was a pleasing sounding fella with a calm personality.

"Just waiting for my interview." Dave pointed out or discussed his general situation.

"What is the name of the firm again?"

"It's called 'Variety Solutions'."

"What is a dumb name?" Simon replied with a critical remark.

"I can see that, but it's the only one I have on my horizon."

"What about the other interviews?"

"I have postponed them for next week. I am solely focusing on tomorrow as of right now."

"Nice, you'll get it. I have a gut feeling."

"Me too."

Simon looked around and smelled the freshly brewed coffee and food items.

"Let's order something." He said as he looked at the menu board above the counter.

"I already did."

"Ok, what did you order?"

"Two coffees and two sandwiches. I hope you don't mind it."

"Nah, it's good. Sandwiches will do for me. Plus, you saved me some money." Simon chuckled.

"Simon, you owe me breakfast now. I would have forgotten, but now you've reminded me."

"Just shut up. You remember the money I owed you in our previous lives. Don't get me started on your big heart."

The two continued back and forth, talking about all the nonsense in their lives. The waiter brought them their breakfast, which looked delicious. However, after some time, the topic of Ella came up, which changed the mood of the two boys.

"I wish things were a bit different," Simon said when talking about the end phase of their college.

"Yes, everything that happened shouldn't have happened. And the worst part is that the parents have to go through it each and every day." Dave took one sip from the cup.

"Dave, I know you don't like to talk about this, but what do you think happened to her?"

"I don't know, and frankly speaking, I don't care anymore." He looked down. "I mean, if something happened to her, I am sorry for everyone's loss, but if she left everyone on purpose, I can never forgive her."

"But why would you say that?" Simon asked. "I mean, you two had a history, but that was in the very beginning." He took a pause. "Is there something you knew about her?"

Dave was mildly frustrated. "Man, what's up with this early morning investigation." Dave lowered his voice as he caught the attention of others in the restaurant. "I had moments with Ella, but I never imagined something like this would happen to her."

Simon sat there still with an eager face as if anticipating more words from his friend.

"What?" Dave gave his friend an angry look.

"Fine, let's leave this behind us." The two of them finished their meals and went back. By then, Dave was back to normal and having a great time with Simon. However, after having a conversation for a couple of hours, Simon left because of some work.

Dave, too, went back to Nick's apartment to nap. He crashed upon reaching the place, and Nick woke him up after returning from his job.

"Dave, are you ok?" Nick asked his cousin, who was still half asleep.

"Yeah, I am fine. I am just a little dizzy."

"What?" Nick paused for a second. "Did you get drunk during the day?"

"No, God, no. I went out with my friend, and the food was too heavy. So, I just got into a nap."

"Well, your nap is now almost a hardworking man's sleep."

"Really, what time is it?" Dave was coming back to his senses.

"Umm, can't you see me in front of you?"

"Oh shit, really. I must've overslept." Dave sounded a little guilty. "I'll freshen up and catch up with you."

Nick nodded and didn't say a word. He left Dave's room. After fifteen minutes, he entered the main hall, where his cousin watched some sports highlights. The clock was almost seven in the evening, and it was time for dinner.

"Davey, what do you need for dinner?" Nick asked as he held his phone in his left hand.

"Are you ordering something?"

"Yes, I don't feel like cooking a meal, so I am looking for something online."

"Don't worry, I can cook something if you want." Dave was hesitant of his offer as he knew about his Michelin-level cooking skills, but it was the least he could do for his tired brother.

"No need for it. I got this. So, what would you like to have?" Nick also knew about Dave's cooking skills, and he, too, wanted none of that.

"Umm, just repeat what you're having." Dave sat on a giant bean bag on the left side of the big sofa.

"Ok." Nick scrolled through his cell and ordered something. "Alright then, two pizzas are on the way.

Dave was not delighted to hear this as he held his bloated stomach from the food he had eaten during the day. But he couldn't say anything since it was his fault to not choose anything when the offer stood.

"So, Dave." Nick muted the television. "Did you complete your required paperwork?"

"Everything is set, and I look forward to tomorrow."

"Great." The man looked back to the screen. "Ok, let's watch a game or two."

Both of them watched the games till their food came. After dinner, Dave went to his room, where he sat studying for the next day. He was nervous but confident at the same time. However, it was not the job that frustrated him; it was something else he couldn't face at the time.

Dave didn't sleep the whole night for obvious reasons. He researched the whole night and just took a nap before heading for his interview. Nick wished him luck before leaving for the office, and now it was all up to Dave to make the most of the opportunity. He freshened up and was ready for the day. His parents also called in the morning to wish him good luck.

He called in a cab for his transport, which took around five minutes to reach his apartment. After double-checking all the documents and important papers, he was set to leave the office. However, things were about to be a little different than he'd expected them to be.

During his taxi journey, Dave passed through a small garden. He was lost in his thoughts, and then, all of a sudden, he saw a similar face. It was none other than Ella's. Dave was in complete shock upon seeing his missing friend. The man even rubbed his eyes and contemplated the situation for a second.

Unfortunately, his vehicle crossed the entire boundary of the small park.

"Sir, can you stop the car for a second." Dave hurriedly asked the driver to park on the side of the pavement. He immediately ran backwards towards the entrance or the main gate—a dome-shaped, iron-framed gate with a petal design.

He entered the park and looked at the different places. Unfortunately, the girl was nowhere to be seen. Maybe it was Dave's illusion. Perhaps he took someone else for Ella.

He was lost in the park for a moment or two but recollected his attention as the thoughts of being late for the interview came to mind. Stunned and struck, Dave returned back to his taxi.

"Everything all right, sir?" Asked the middle-aged male driver with a blue cap.

"Yes, everything is just fine." Dave looked at him. "I am sorry for causing trouble and wasting your time."

"No problem, sir. It happens." The driver started the cab and took Dave to his destination. Dave paid an additional tip for his mid-journey nuisance.

He entered the Variety Solutions Inc. building. It was a triple-storey glass build structure with solar panels alongside windows.

After entering the office, Dave went to different rounds of interviews and corporate formalities. Luckily, the man's credentials were almost perfect for the job, and later that day, he was selected for the designer role. However, Dave only had one thought in his mind, and it was seeing Ella at the park.

III

Moving Back

Dave's life was in a weird place. On the one hand, everyone congratulated him for getting his first job. His friends and family were showering him with blessings. However, Dave was still thinking about Ella, whom he had seen in the garden. His mind can't fathom the fact that it could all be a big, giant illusion or misconception.

After reaching the apartment, Dave switched off his phone; he wanted to leave the phoniness of his acquaintances and focus on the earlier part of the day.

"Am I intoxicated?" Dave thought to himself as he lay on his bed. He was watching the fan circling around the wooden ceiling. The paint on the walls came from some places and made an intricate pattern.

Dave was lost in his thoughts, and before he could think further, he was asleep. It was afternoon, so there was still plenty of time to calm his mind for a bit.

His cousin came back from the office and woke him up.

"Dave, wake up, it's already dark outside." Nick shook him gently, and he came back to his senses. His eyes were red, and he was sweating like a varsity athlete.

"You all right." Nick looked at his brother. "Seems like you've been in a war in your dreams."

"Nah, it's just–leave it. I'll freshen up." Dave got up to take a shower.

"Hey, also my aunt called." Nick looked around. "She tried to reach you."

"My bad, my phone is dead. I'll call her later."

"Alright."

Nick was still standing in front of the door, which was a bit odd. He was looking at Dave as if he was missing something.

"What do you want?" Dave looked confusingly at his cousin.

"Really, you want me to say it?"

"Say what?"

"You got a job today. You need to buy me a drink."

"Oh, sorry, I am just–it's been a long day. Alright, wherever you want to go."

"Now you're talking."

Nick was excited to have some drinks for the night. However, he didn't have any idea what was going on in Dave's mind. They decided to have a drink or two in a nearby club. He even invited Simon as well.

They all reached a nearby club named "Sunshine". Ironically, there was not even a moonlight at the place as it was stacked with people. Even though it was a weekday, there were plenty of people dancing and drinking.

Dave was lost in his thoughts. He thought maybe a couple of drinks might help him to come back to his senses. Nick and Simon started to dance after some drinks. Both of them knew how to party as if it was another day in the office for them. Meanwhile, Dave was drinking like an alcoholic, and there was no one to stop him.

He looked around the bar, and there were flashy lights, girls in dresses, drunk people and loud music. An hour passed, and there were no signs of anyone stopping. It was getting really nauseous inside the place, and Dave decided to smoke outside. He carried a drink in his hand all the way to the outside street. Luckily, he didn't spill the drink, and there were no police around. He lit a cigarette while holding a drink in his left hand.

A moment passed, and people came and left the place. Dave sat on the sidewalk as he saw the different faces, all excited to visit the club. However, as he gazed across the road, he saw Ella—standing in her attire, looking directly into Dave's eyes. For a moment, the man couldn't move, think or even react. He immediately put aside his drink, stood up and ran across the road towards the girl. But as soon as he took his first, a car came and slightly hit Dave, leaving him imbalanced and folded on the road.

The people saw this and rushed toward the fallen guy. The security guards immediately took him to the side of the road and away from the club. Luckily, one of them recognised him and called his friends immediately from inside.

Both Nick and Simon came out and, upon seeing their pal on the pavement, rushed immediately to his aid.

"What happened?" Nick asked the security.

"Sir, he just stepped on the road and a car hit him. To his luck, he was safe and not badly hurt."

"Simon, we need to take him to the hospital. Maybe his arm is broken."

"Yes, I think so."

Dave was half-conscious, but in his mind, he was still thinking about Ella. Simon rushed immediately to his car and brought it in front of the club. The two security guards helped them to place the victim in the back seat. Nick, too, sat with him. Simon was rushed to the nearby hospital. At that point, Dave was getting an idea about the whole situation.

"She's alive." Dave muttered in his mouth.

"What did you say?" Nick had no idea what he said at that moment.

"Do you think he hurt his head?" Simon asked as he looked back at his friend.

"Nah, I don't think so; maybe he got too drunk."

"Don't worry, Nick, we'll reach the hospital soon."

"Yeah, right."

Nick sighed as he looked outside, wondering about the situation and gazing at the well-lit buildings.

They reached the hospital and admitted Dave. The man was examined by an emergency doctor who was working the night shift. He, alongside two nurses, looked into the matter for a couple of hours.

The doctor came, who held his coat on the left elbow. He was short, bald, with a lean build. He kind of reminded Nick of his friend. Simon was outside at that moment.

"You must be Nick?" The doctor shook Nick's hand. "Are you with Dave?"

"Yes, is he all right?"

"Yeah, he's fine, just a bit concussed, that's all." The doctor looked at his watch. "Let him rest for a couple of hours, and then you can take him back."

"Alright, sir, thank you very much." Nick was eased.

The doctor took off after gently tapping Nick's shoulders. It was assuring, and now Nick can take a breath of relief. Soon after, Simon came too. He was a bit hungover from a few hours, but he brought two cups of coffee with him. He handed one to Nick, who thanked him and nodded at him with an appreciative smile.

"What did the doctor say?" Simon asked as they stood in front of Nick. "I saw him outside at a small shop for a smoke."

"Well he said that Dave is fine, he just needs to rest for a bit."

"Thank God, it could've been worse for him." He paused with a sigh of relief. "And all of us. I don't even want to think about it."

Nick didn't say much after. After finishing his coffee, he went over to the reception to complete the hospital formalities. It took some time, and afterwards, Nick asked Simon to go back, but the man refused. He wanted to go back with Dave and make sure that he was safe and sound.

The night passed as both Nick and Simon scrolled through their phones, waiting for the hospital to discharge Dave as soon as he was awake. In the early morning, Dave was back to his senses and ready to leave. There were minor injuries on his forearm and a small band-aid on his forehead. Other than that, he was fine and calm. He, too, was drunk, and it was clearly visible in his body language—he was slow and stiff as if stuck in the mud.

Nick helped him to get outside, where Simon was waiting for him in his car. After carefully settling in the vehicle, all three of them drove back to the apartment. Dave was still nauseous, and his cousin had to take leave from the office, considering the situation. Simon, too, went to his home and promised Dave he would visit in the evening.

No one told Dave's parents about the event, and they all decided that it was best to leave it that way. After settling Dave in his room, Nick decided to rest all day. He was not hungry, and neither was Dave. The whole day elapsed, with two of them lying on their beds. It was 5 PM, and Dave was perfectly fine. He got up and saw that Nick was still resting. So, without disturbing him, he got outside to take a stroll through the locality.

At that time, he was greeted by Simon, who was a bit stressed when he saw Dave outside.

"Hey Simon." He greeted his friend on the stairs.

"What are you doing outside?" Simon asked worriedly. "You should get some rest."

"Nah, I am good. I just wanted some fresh air." He continued moving downstairs, and Simon was following him. "I've been in bed all day." They moved along the street.

"So what?" Simon was confused. "Didn't the doctor tell you to rest for a couple of days."

"True, but he doesn't know everything?"

"What do you mean?" Simon asked confusingly.

"Simon." Dave stopped and looked at his friend. "I need to tell you something, but you must promise me that you won't judge it."

"Yeah sure. I won't. I promise." The curiosity grew in Simon's eyes.

"I saw Ella."

"Wait, what?" He took a pause. "What do you mean by that?"

"The day before yesterday, when I was on my way to the firm, I saw Ella entering a local park. I got out to make sure, but she was not there. At first, I thought that it was just a misunderstanding. I kept thinking about her all that day. And yesterday, outside the club, I saw her again." Dave was breathing heavily as if he was tired all of a sudden. "She was on the other side of the road—staring right at me. Maybe I was too drunk, but I swear to God it was her."

"So that's why you were hit when crossing the road?"

Dave nodded, but Simon didn't say a word for a bit. He was taking his time to settle the story in his mind.

Simon looked at Dave. "But what if it's all a delusion? I mean she's missing and it's been over a year. Are you sure it was her?"

"I wish but after seeing her again the previous day. I don't know to be honest. And I don't know what to do now?"

"What do you mean? You have a job now, so do it and try to leave it behind. What else do you want to hear?"

"But what if I saw her again?"

Simon was trying his best to keep the conversation rational. "Dave, I don't know what you saw but I can only advise you to keep it behind you and move on. I know you and Ella were close at some point in your lives but she's gone and a few days back, I don't think you cared about her. And now all of a sudden—you're just not normal."

"I guess you're right but I need to look into the matter."

Simon was not pleased to hear that. "And how are you supposed to do this?"

"Maybe I should go back to Pinewood and look into the case."

"Are you stupid? Why the hell do you want to do that?"

"I had to–it's important for me." Dave replied confidently.

"Really, and what about your career?"

"I don't care about it at the moment."

"Dave, I don't know if you can hear yourself. But you sound really stupid. Why would you ever do that?"

"Because I have to." There was no point in arguing with Dave as he already made up his mind.

"She's not real." Simon tried his best for the last time but failed miserably. Dave didn't argue more about it. Seeing Dave's stance, Simon decided that there was no point in discussing the situation further. Therefore, without saying a word, he left and went back to his car, which was parked on the next street.

Dave, too, went back to his apartment, where he saw Nick still resting and taking complete naps. Seeing his cousin in deep sleep, Dave decided to book his tickets back to Pinewood. He also notified his company that he wouldn't be able to join them at the moment. It was something that the people at the firm didn't appreciate. But Dave couldn't care less for them. He didn't know them, so it was nothing to him.

As far as his family was concerned, he told them he was again enrolling in a small course which would take a couple of months. And after that, he will seek out a job once again. It was something that his parents didn't understand, but they didn't even compel him on his decision. For them, Dave knew more about his endeavours than they did.

Once Nick woke, Dave also shared the news with him. And his reaction was similar to most of the rest.

"What is this program?" Nick was not buying the stuff Dave made up.

"Nothing, it's just a type of workshop which will boost my skills."

"Who told you about it?"

"I only received mail from my college today."

Nick was suspicious and demanded evidence. "Really, can I see it?"

"Yeah sure."

Dave handed his cell to his brother, who looked at the mail. After a few brief seconds, he handed it back.

"Alright." The dubious look on his face turned into satisfaction. "When are you leaving?"

"Tomorrow at early morning."

"You said it will take two months."

"Yes, but it all depends on my timing to complete the program."

"Ok." Nick took a deep breath as if he was restarting his body after sleeping the whole day. "I don't know Dave what you're doing? But if these couple of months will help you in your career then you're good to go. As far as I am concerned, you're making the wrong move. I mean, you already got your job so I don't think you should go back to studies."

"You're probably right but this logic goes the same way to my studies. I will not get any chance to do this again in the future. So, I might take it."

Nick nodded in an agreeing manner. "Fair enough. Best of luck and let me know if you need any help."

"Thanks, I appreciate it."

"And what happened yesterday," Nick said in a serious tone, "That stays with the three of us forever."

"Got it," Dave replied, and Nick went to do his own chores.

"I am glad I didn't delete that summer program mail from my inbox." Dave thought as he was packing his stuff in a big bag. His train was in the morning, and there was still some time left before he could meet Simon. He wanted to say goodbye plus ensure that his pal kept his secret from everyone.

Apparently, Simon was busy with some work and didn't pick up his cell. Therefore, Dave decided to leave a text message explaining his situation, and that was it for him for the day. The man was ready to go back, and now it was just a matter of time before he set foot once again in the place that unexpectedly came back to haunt him.

It was early morning, and Nick dropped his cousin off at the railway station. After bidding farewell to Nick, Dave was ready to face what was ahead of him.

IV
Nothing Changes

Upon reaching Pinewood, Dave needed a place to stay, and he tried to reach Elliot to see if he was in town. Luckily, Elliot was at home and was glad to hear from Dave. It's been a tense situation between the two after Ella went missing. However, both were willing to settle their differences and renew their years of friendship.

Elliot called Dave at his house, where he was greeted by Mrs Grant. She was a lovely lady, short with long dark hair and a glowing broad smile on a round face. Elliot looked a lot like her when it comes to facial expressions. She was dressed up and welcomed her guest. Soon after, Elliot came out of his room as well.

It's been a while since both of them saw each other. Elliot grew a dense beard—making it hard to recognise him.

"How are you doing?" Both of them hugged each other, which was more of a forgiveness gesture.

"How is everything, Davey?" Mrs Grant poured two glasses of water into a white tray.

"I am great, just in town for some academic work."

"Oh really, what is it?"

"Just an art program. I am thinking about signing up for it."

"Well, that's great." She took a seat. "But I thought you were looking for a job in the city."

"Yes, it was my plan, but I dropped the idea because I may not get an opportunity like this in the future. You know, once you're working, it's nearly impossible to get time for such skill-gaining endeavours."

"You're right. Me and Elliot were discussing the same topic the other day."

Dave needed clarification. "Pardon me, but are you also looking for a job?" He looked at his friend.

"I was thinking about it but I don't want to rush anything. I want to grab a job here in town only. And administration is my only option."

"Good for you. I know you can easily get that position."

"Thanks for the optimism, but it's a little harder than I expected."

"Everything in life worthwhile requires effort." Dave with some words of wisdom.

"You're right about that."

"Listen Elliot, I have to go now." Mrs Grant stood up as it was her time to go to the office. "You take care of your friend. Have a nice day Dave, I'll see you in the evening."

"Sure Mrs Grant. You too."

Mrs Grant left, and now, only the two friends were there. However, the smile on Elliot's face vanished as soon as his mother left.

Dave looked at his friend with a serious face. "What's wrong?"

"Simon called me last night and told me everything." Elliot stood up. "Listen Dave, I don't agree for you to stay with me because you were my friend. I did so because I owed you some favours from the past. I don't care what you think or want to do here? I just want you gone from my sight as soon as possible. You have three days. Get your place and never return."

Dave broke his silence. "Elliot, but listen to me. She's alive."

"See there." Elliot closed his fist and banged the wall. Dave was shaking and didn't say anything further. "I don't want any part of this. So just comfort yourself and let me move on in my life. You need food; it's in the refrigerator."

Elliot went to his room angrily. He was still pissed at Dave and his sudden appearance, and there was nothing Dave could say or do to change his friend's mind. He sat on the chair for a bit—thinking about everything.

He was alone in a town that was once his home. He couldn't believe that he sacrificed his present for a call from the past. Now, it was only he who needed to do some investigation on the matter.

Thinking about all this, Dave fell asleep on the chair. It was still early in the morning, and Dave was accustomed to sleeping throughout the day. After three hours, the sound of a horn wakes him up, and he sees Elliot standing in front of him. It scared him a bit.

"What are you doing?" Dave came back to his senses.

"Nothing I am just checking on you." Elliot took a step back. "You were murmuring something in your sleep."

"It was just a bad dream." Dave sank his head in his two hands.

Elliot looked at him. "All life is just a dream where people are waiting to wake up." He chucked a bit. "Here, drink some water. And if you want to sleep, you can go into the guest room."

"Alright. Thanks."

Elliot went inside his room. Meanwhile, Dave was just wondering about his vague dream. To his surprise, he did not remember anything apart from the fact that he was alone in the town looking for something.

He drank some water and freshened up. Without anything, he took his bag and left Elliot's place. It was the right decision on his part, as there was no need for him to create a fuss at his house.

He contacted one of the local brokers to help him find a nice place somewhere in the town. It was already afternoon, and the Sun was not being nice to him. Fortunately, his broker called him to meet at the locality, and there were some apartments that Dave could check out.

The place was called WestWard Locals and was on the outskirts of Pinewood town. However, everything was really cheap there, so it was probably an ideal deal for someone like Dave, who had less budget.

He visited the place carrying his luggage. There, he met Patrick, who was the broker and owner of the small apartment.

"How are you doing, sir?" Patrick, a tall guy with a wide frame and a tall hairstyle, greeted Dave. He was wearing a white shirt tucked in his long pants. His dark, lean face was filled with a beard, while his goggles covered his eyes.

"I am good, so this is the place?" Dave was astonished upon looking at the place. It was not too big, but it could easily accommodate a couple of people. On top of that, it was secluded from the rest of the buildings. So, it was great for personal investigation and research. Since Pinewood was not a big place, getting a small apartment was not hectic. Also, Dave knew the guy from his graduation years. He rented a place during his first semester for a couple of months.

"Yes?" Replied Patrick, who was, for some reason, wearing his shades inside the apartment. He held his phone in his right hand as if eagerly waiting for some reply.

"Alright. Let me look around." Dave strolled through the two rooms and a small kitchen and looked at the furnishing. He liked the place as it was ideal for Dave's stay, and without even thinking about it, he rented the whole place. It cost him a lot, but it was better to stay away from Elliot and his family.

"So, can I finalise this place?" Patrick asked eagerly.

"Yes, sure." Dave looked around a bit. "I like it."

"Thank you. I will take care of the legal formalities for you. You can stay here and set yourself up."

"I appreciate it Patrick."

Dave arranged his stuff inside the room and sat on a small chair; Patrick left the place with money in his wallet. He even seemed a bit surprised by the instant decision-making of his old tenant. But he couldn't care less about him as he was busy with the other stuff as well.

Dave was sitting in his newly occupied place, thinking about the future. He was here based on a lie, and only a couple of people knew about his secret investigation plan. Now, all he needed was to look into the matter by himself and start as soon as possible.

He didn't want to waste a single day. So, right away, he started looking at all the potential information that the authorities had on the case. Since it was a private investigation—there were not a lot of resources at Dave's disposal. On top of that, he was just a novice with an intrinsic call to look into Ella's past.

Dave started looking into the records, online articles, statements and journalist's analysis. As expected, there were not a lot of details on the case.

He needed to start from the ground level in hopes of building the case. His only reference to any sort of investigation came from dozens of crime movies, which he enjoyed during his graduation. And now, it was time to put these fictional theories into practice.

It was late, and Dave was still trying his best to lay some foundation after starting the whole thing. He got a call from Elliot. Dave replied and explained everything about his whereabouts after leaving his home.

Elliot was not happy on behalf of his mother about Dave's act of not informing them. However, he was glad that he no longer had to be a part of his act. He hung up the phone after a few minutes and was ready to cut off any links with his former friend.

Dave expected it and, without any more confrontation, got back to his work. He was still in touch with Simon, who was trying to assist him with any sort of help. He was grateful for him, at least.

Hours passed, and it was getting dark in Pinewood. It was the beginning of the winter season, and there were a lot of bright lights on the street alongside cold, shivering but pleasant air. Dave decided to visit Ella's parents to check out the place that was the root of the incident.

He walked to the street where Ella lived. The place had a lot of memories, which were once bright, but now, they are all dark and painful. Even Dave took a step back as he tried to approach the house. With the remaining courage, he entered the porch and knocked on the door.

A voice came from inside, which was not resembling. "Give me a second." A short, old white lady, around 80, with curly hair, opened the door. She wore a grey granny dress, and her face lit up when he saw Dave.

For a second, Dave looked at the sign on the right side of the door. It was the same address; however, he didn't expect someone else to show.

"Good evening ma'am." He greeted her.

"Thank god, you're here. Come inside, I am having a rough day with television. I called dozens of times in your office but it took you the whole day to show up."

The old lady mistook Dave for some engineer, which she had been expecting. Dave, too, decided to play his part in this misunderstanding, as it was easier for him to understand what the hell was happening in the first place.

She took him to the old television, which was stuttering a lot. "Here it is; it's been like this the whole day." The lady sat on the sofa in front of the chair. "I don't know if it's some button that I pressed, but I hope it is a minor problem.

"Don't worry, ma'am." Dave crouched in front of the television. "Give me a second." He looked behind the television and saw that the wire was a bit loose. He immediately knew what was wrong with the machine. However, he decided to take his time.

"Ma'am." I forgot my tool kit. "Do you have any sort of plier by any chance?"

The lady went into deep thinking as if remembering something. "Wait here, let me bring you my husband's kit. Maybe you'll find something useful there."

She left the room and came back with a small kit. It had almost every necessary tool in it. Dave took a plier out of it—it was rusty and full of dirt.

In the meantime, the lady went into the kitchen to bring some water while Dave just adjusted and tightened the two wires into the TV plug. He restarted the system, and it was good to go.

However, the thing was so loud that it hurt Dave's ears. He had to shut down the entire thing and adjust the volume before starting it again. The old lady came back hurriedly after listening to the whole noise. "Did you fix it?"

"Yes, it's almost done."

After lowering the volume, Dave started the television, and it was good to go. He kept all the things safely in the toolkit and grabbed the cold glass of water that the lady had kept on the small table in front of him.

"Thank you dear." There was a smile on her face. "So, how much do I pay you?"

"It's nothing. You're good."

"Really?"

"Yes, umm, we are paid by the firm for customer complaints. There's no need."

"That's very nice of you and your firm." She replied. However, Dave still had his questions, which required some answers.

"You must be new here because last time, the Cooper family used to live here?"

"Yes, you're right. I moved in here with my husband a few weeks back. Originally, we are from the South City."

"South City? Well, that's a long way back home."

"It is pretty far from here but we wanted a peaceful place—considering our age and health." She had one eye fixed on the television. "Plus, the property is reasonably cheap here."

"Good for you." Dave nodded with a small smile. "Umm, do you know what happened to the Coopers? I mean why did they leave the town?"

She looked back at him. "The Cooper family? I don't know the whole story, but I guess it was their daughter." She leaned as if somebody was listening to him. "You might have heard about their daughter."

"Yes, a very unfortunate situation," Dave replied remorsefully.

"Right, I guess they didn't enjoy living here. So, they just left. I can see things might not be going well between them as well. But who knows?"

"Did you know where they went or transferred?" Dave asked curiously.

"Wish I had an answer to that but as I said earlier. I didn't know them. I only heard about them from my real estate agent. His name is Harvey. A great guy—helped me a lot to move in here."

"Alright, no worries. I am just curious. You know—I just wondered about them." Dave was not convinced, but he couldn't expect much from the old lady. He decided to leave the house and work further on his investigation.

"I must leave now. I hope your television works well in the future."

"Thank you, dear, for coming. God bless you." The old lady had a big smile on her face.

Dave left the place. He didn't even ask the old lady her name, but it didn't matter. He knew about the Cooper family. However, he still needs to know their location. Maybe something came up, and it was too hard for them to digest, leaving them in an unfortunate situation.

Now, once again, Dave was on the streets. He had no idea what to do next? He'd probably get in touch with the real estate agent, as mentioned by the old lady. Maybe Patrick knows about the guy. He texted him to get the details about the Harvey guy mentioned by the old lady. On the other hand, it was getting late and dark, and there were little to no people on the small streets of Pinewood.

He grabbed some hot broth for dinner and was on his way back. However, he got a call from Simon, who was worried about his whereabouts. It was obvious that everything Dave was doing was based on a small faith. A faith that his friend was still alive. However, everyone else who knew about his secret came to a different conclusion. Simon, per se, was in the middle of a situation far beyond his apprehension. He wanted to help his friend, but either way, he'd end up causing trouble for himself.

But still, he wanted to play his part in the whole act so as to keep Dave out of trouble after learning that Dave already found a place and settled in Pinewood. He asked Dave to be part of the investigation. More eyes are merrier—considering that the whole situation is a hypothesis.

The news sounded splendid to Dave's eyes and ears as he couldn't be more grateful to have someone behind his back.

After hanging up, Dave visited an old place. It was an elevated spot, a bit outside of the main town and at a high elevation. From there, one can see the lights around the area. It was a place close to Dave, where he used to come with Ella. He even grabbed a drink there with Elliot at some point when they were close friends. But now everything has changed, and there is nothing Dave can do in his power to get those moments back again.

He sat there—watched the city lights, and enjoyed his hot meal. It was a long day for him as now his tired body was in search of some rest. Considering that his place was a bit too far, he decided to lie down on a small bench under the shining stars. It was very cold, but Dave was used to such low temperatures.

V
Tragedies of The Past

Dave called Elliot after Ella went missing. It was right after Elliot stormed out of the whole scene. He felt ashamed on Elliot's behalf in front of the Cooper family. Something was not right and it was bothering his friend.

Elliot didn't want to indulge in the ongoing investigation at the time. Not only that, Dave, too, was shaken apart from the whole situation. So much so that he started to look around for his friend who, all of a sudden, vanished or disappeared into the thin air.

Elliot was at his home; he needed some alone time to get back to his senses. However, Dave needed someone to aid him. So, without thinking much, he visited Elliot, who sat on a couch in a depressed mood.

Dave entered with his own sadness. "Hey, how are you doing?" He sat across from Elliot but didn't speak for a bit.

"Why did you leave? And don't give me your previous excuse?"

"Dave, I can't handle such a situation. I don't know how to react. I thought I was tough, but I am not that guy." Elliot broke the silence and continued. "She was partying with us a few days ago." There were tears in his eyes. "We all were celebrating and looking forward to the future, but I've never thought that something like this would happen. It's heart-wrenching, and I can't take it."

"But you can't be like this! People need you now more than ever. And Ella needs you." Dave exclaimed. "I need you, we can help in searching for her."

"Ah, leave it. We can't do anything. You think you're an expert." Elliot goes off on his friend. "You think you can find her with your art expertise."

"We can try, man." Dave insisted, but Elliot was stubborn, and maybe he made sense. "It's the least we can do for her." Dave with one last appeal.

"I am sorry Dave, I can't help you." He replied remorsefully. "Let me be, I don't need anyone around me."

Dave left Elliot, and it was the beginning of the end for their true friendship. After the incident began to settle down, they met on a couple of occasions, but things were never the same—Elliot started focusing on his own career, and Dave, too, was busy with his exams at the college. Even in the present, none of them expect much of each other.

Dave felt a chilling drop on his right cheek. It woke him up, and immediately, he came back to his senses. He was asleep on the bench. It was midnight, and there were clouds all over town. The wind was blowing, and it was freezing all around. He grabbed his coat and mobile phone as soon as possible; there might be some light drizzles in Pinewood.

As Dave was on his way to his apartment, he saw a shadowy figure across the road. It was a frightening experience since he knew who it was. However, as soon as

Dave tried to point some light on Ella using his phone, she was gone—leaving him with the memories or the tragedies of the past. He was starting to contemplate his sanity and the whole reality around him.

The rain was beginning to spread the aroma of sand around the town. It was one of those scents which you enjoy when reading or looking out of the window.

There were still some people on the streets, some of them taking cover in the shelters. However, Dave decided not to stop and to reach his place as soon as possible. He took some advanced and pacey steps towards his destination. And when he arrived at his apartment, he was almost fully wet. His shivering was visible all around the body. He quickly changed his clothes, dried himself off and got some hot mocha for the cold or flu. After all this, he got in his bed and was finally at the place where he was supposed to be.

The next day, it was early, and Dave received a call from Simon. He arrived at Pinewood and asked for his address so he could get on his way to Dave's apartment.

In the meantime, Dave decided to get some breakfast for his guest. He had been feeling a little sick since last night. But he already took some precautionary medication for his aid.

It was 8 in the morning, and the doorbell rang. Dave opened the door, and Simon entered. He looked around for a bit and found a place to keep his bag.

They both hugged, and Dave was relieved to see his friend. "You finally came?" Said Dave with a sigh of relief.

"I mean, I can't let you lose your mind alone in this place," Simon said, taunting his friend.

"Speaking of that?" Dave got serious. "I saw her again last night. It was late and she was in the city."

"Dave, we spoke about this." Simon took a seat. "Listen, I am not here because I believe your story but because I believe in our friendship. I want to help you in any way possible." He continued. "So, if you want to investigate this matter. I am here with you but you must promise me that you will return back to the city if all roads lead towards a dead end." Simon lowered his voice as if speaking with sincerity. "Can you promise me that?"

"Alright, pal." Dave took his hand out of his pocket to shake hands with his friend. "I hear you, and I promise to return home."

"Thank you." Simon took a deep breath. "So, did you have anything on this case?"

"Na, nothing much. The last day was rough. I left Elliot's place to find this apartment. And in the evening I decided to visit the Cooper family. However, they have left Pinewood."

"You mean, they sold their house."

"Seems like it, now an old lady lives there."

"That's unexpected. But where did they go?"

"I don't know but we'll find their location today." Dave said confidently. "I'll talk to the real estate agent who sold the old lady their house. He'll probably know where the Coopers are gone?"

"Well, that's a start." Simon nodded in agreement.

Dave went to the kitchen. "But before that, I have some cereal which we can have for breakfast. After that, let's meet that estate agent."

"Sounds good to me," Simon said in a relaxed tone.

Both of them had some breakfast and also some conversation about the case. Dave had doubts about Simon showing up at his door, but he didn't want to bother himself with that thought. He needed an additional hand for the investigation, and Simon was a trustworthy name.

They both made some calls after their meals and found out about the real estate agent. His name was Harvey, and his office was located on Mall Street. They decided to give him a visit during his office hours. But there were some questions from Simon which bothered Dave.

"Dave, I don't get it." Simon looked confused.

"What are you talking about?"

"If you want to know about Ella's parents, why don't you call them? I am pretty sure you're in touch with them."

"I thought of it at first, but then I couldn't make any moves that didn't look suspicious. I want to make our visit as natural as possible."

"But what if they are pretty far from here. Then what will you do?"

"Frankly, I don't know, and I don't care at the moment." He paused. "I just need to find their location, that's it. We'll figure something out from there."

They both got ready to visit Harvey and travelled for twenty-five minutes. They reached the man's office. It was a pretty busy place, considering the early time of the day. They waited at the reception as Harvey was in some meeting. The receptionist informed Harvey about the two young guys who wanted to see him.

After half an hour, they were escorted to his bright office by a small lady in formal attire. Her hair was set together, and she wore a large spec on her pointy face.

"This way." The two followed her until they reached Harvey's desk—he was a middle-aged man with short grey hair, a bit fat and a densely bearded face. He wore a white shirt and blue pants and was on a call. He gestured to wait for him for two seconds, and then he dropped his call.

Harvey stood up from his chair. "Please, have a seat." All of them sat. "Jennifer, can you bring us some coffee?"

The lady went outside to fetch the drinks but left the door open on her way.

"So, how can I help you guys?" Harvey asked with a broad smile.

"We won't take much of your time but we just want to know about the Cooper family." Dave said formally.

"Cooper family?" He thought for a bit. "Who used to live on the North end of Pinewood—near that old garage?"

"Yes, that's the one. Do you know where they went?" Simon added with great enthusiasm.

"Ok, but who are you?" Harvey got defensive all of a sudden.

"We were friends with her daughter. It's been a long time since we saw them so that's why we're looking for them."

"Hmmm." He stood up and walked towards the table to fetch some files. "I helped Mr and Mrs Cooper to sell their house to the Edmonds. But that's all. I don't know where they went."

"Are you serious? It never came up in any of your conversations." Simon pressed with an interrogative tone.

"Excuse me sir, but I am not obliged to answer you. Are you from the police?" Harvey was pissed at Simon as he closed the file and kept it back on the table. Dave sensed the rising tension in the room and tried to change the situation of the place. He gestured to Simon to take things slowly and respectfully.

"I apologise on behalf of my friend. The thing is we want to meet them. So, it'll be very helpful if you remember anything about them."

"I already said I don't know exactly but at one instance I can recall that they were conversing about buying some place in Silver Lake town. But again I am not 100 percent certain."

Dave stood up. "Alright, thank you for your time." Simon gave Harvey a despising look.

"How'd you guys know about me?"

"Patrick told me about you." Dave replied. "Do you know him?"

"Patrick, yes, he's an old associate of mine. Good guy."

"Sure he is. Alright then." Dave said with a broad smile. "Thank you for your time."

The two left the office and were on the streets. Simon started right away. "He knew about them. He's lying and full of crap."

"I know Simon but we can't create a scene here as we want to keep authorities out of this for as long as possible. So, please don't be so provocative and just shut up. Do you understand?"

Simon took a deep breath. "You're right. That was not the right thing to do."

"So, do you believe him? Silver Lake. That's pretty far from here."

"I can't tell but it could be possible."

"Are you really going to put your bets on that lying agent inside? What if he informs them."

"For now, I am uncertain and helpless, but don't worry; I have some acquaintances in Silver Lake. They might help us?"

"Who?" Simon looked confused.

"Do you remember Aadi?"

"That intern who came during the student exchange program."

"Yes, you're right. He lived with us for a couple of months."

"Wait, you're still in touch with him?"

"Yes." Dave smiled.

"He's from Silver Lake?"

"He used to live there but I don't know about the present. But still he can be a great help to us?"

"I mean, you're not wrong." Simon looked down the streets, thinking about the situation. "So, when will you call him?"

"I will but first let's get a cup of coffee. I need some peaceful place before reaching out to him."

The two of them entered a local cafe, took a small seat by the window and ordered two big cups of latte. It's been quite cold in the town lately because of the rain for the past couple of days. Dave took out his cell and looked for Aadi's number. He called him, but the guy didn't pick up his phone.

Simon looked at his friend, who tried again. "Everything all good?"

"Yeah, maybe he's busy. I'll try again."

Both of them sat waiting for their order, as none of them wanted to have small talk. A few minutes passed, and a loud noise came. It was Simon's cell who stood up from his seat and excused his friend. Dave was so desperate for a callback that he kept on checking his phone consistently. Even though their order came from one of the slowest serviced restaurants, his phone was deadbeat.

Simon returned after taking the call and sat in front of Dave, taking a good inhale of the hot coffee.

"Who was it?" Dave asked curiously.

"Ah, nobody, just a call from one of my associates." Simon evaded the question.

"Associates?" Dave looked at him doubtfully. "Are you working on something?"

Simon was speechless but was saved by Dave's ringing cell. Apparently, Aadi called back, and now it was Dave who took a leave of absence from the table. The call lasted for about five minutes, and when Dave came back to his seat, he was comparatively relieved.

"I told him about the case and the Cooper family."

"Oh nice, what does he say?"

"He told me that he can look into it but he needs some time."

Simon put down his mug. "We have time."

"Yeah, we can wait for some time but I hope he speeds up. It's necessary for us to know the whereabouts of Ella's parents."

Simon nodded in agreement. "Let's suppose we find them—then what? We're going to see them or something? What do we say?"

"I don't know, but before that, we need to investigate some more things here in the town."

"Like what?"

"Things like Ella's disappearance."

"You mean you want to see the police records."

"If I get hold of them." Dave said with a straight face.

"Are you crazy?" Simon looked at Dave astonishingly. "Why'd they give you those files?"

"I will ask them?"

"Wait, are you listening to yourself and what you're saying? I thought you wanted to keep the police out of this case."

"Yes, that's one of our priorities but we need to see where the official investigation ended."

"I think we both know the answer to that?" Simon was pretty confused. "They shut down the case due to the lack of evidence. I mean Ella just vanished into thin air. So, I don't think those files have anything important in them."

"You don't know that Simon. There were a lot of things which were happening at the time and maybe something was kept hidden for a long time."

"Alright. Let's assume you're on to something but how do we get our hands on those files?"

"I know someone who can help with the official work."

"Who?" Simon asked eagerly.

"Are you done with the coffee?"

"Yes but answer my question first?"

"Hurry up! I'll show you."

They both left the shop after paying for their orders at the counter. Simon was both curious and confused as he didn't have any idea about Dave's scheme. But without asking many questions and muttering about the present situation, he decided to follow his friend.

The two took a cab towards the old road street. Dave made the taxi stop at an old double-storey apartment. It seemed like a worn-out residential place.

"You sure this is the place?" Simon asked Dave as they both stood outside. Dave looked around and walked up the pavement towards the front door. He knocked a couple of times before some man responded. After a couple of minutes, a tall young man, fair-skinned, opened the door. He had a thick beard and messy hair. It seemed that he was in the middle of something, and the two hindered his work.

"Can I help you with something?"

"Yes, I am looking for Detective Blake?" Dave responded as Simon stood right behind him."

"You're talking to him."

"I need your help with one case?"

"What case?" Blake asked in an annoyed tone.

"It's complicated. Can we talk about it inside?"

Blake thought for a second. He was still in his shorts, and it was freezing outside. He was in no mood to stand on the door's edge and get smacked by the cold breeze.

"Alright. Come inside."

The two entered the old apartment. It was opposite to its outer appearance, and both of them were astonished to see the compact, cosy and well-lit inside of the apartment. Blake went to his room to put on a sleeping robe. He seemed tired but came back with a cup of coffee and sat across from the two men.

"So, what do you want from me?" He asked as if he couldn't care less for the two.

"Detective Blake, I know you don't know us, but I have heard a lot about you," Dave replied. "You might know my friend Aadi from Silver Lake Town."

Blake was alerted. "Oh, yes. I know him. He helped me with a case back in Silver Lake."

"I am one of his acquaintances from the college."

"Alright. So, what brings you here?"

"Mr Blake, I want you to get details about the case of a missing girl."

Blake chucked. "What, you know that's not your job."

"Yes, but I want to know what happened during the investigation."

"I wish I could help but even if I could, I am no longer associated with the police department." Blake replied disappointingly.

"That's why we're here." Blake continued. "You were one of the best officers in the whole region. And I know that you're doing your own stuff but I know you can help me."

Blake thought for a second. "Which case are you talking about?"

"Ella Cooper! She went missing almost a year back but I believe I saw her couple of days ago. And she didn't seem dead or missing to me at all."

"I probably heard about it." Blake stood from his seat. "Wait a second." He went inside to get something.

Simon looked at Dave in confusion, and Blake came back with a file. He opened it and put it in front of Dave.

"Are you talking about her?" It was Ella's photograph.

"Yes." Dave paused for a bit. "Are you working on this case?"

"I was supposed to as her mother came to me one day, but before I was to start my investigation—his father refused. I don't know what happened. Maybe it's financial or something, but that was it. She never called back for the case. And since I already had plenty of cases to work on, I, too didn't bother to get in trouble on this one."

The room went silent for a few moments. Dave was thinking about the Coopers, who had almost hired a private investigator for Ella but had declined at the last moment.

"When was this?"

"Almost 9 or 10 months back I guess." Blake continued. "Listen, Mr-?"

"I am Dave."

"Dave, I can get you files on this case, but it will cost you money. Look, I am a private detective now, and I can't afford to grant favours in this economy. So, if you want any sort of help or assistance, you have to pay."

"No problem." Dave stood from his seat. "Just get me those files and I'll keep my end of the deal."

The two shook hands and exchanged their numbers. It was beneficial for Dave to have an expert as well, as the case might get more complex than it seemed.

VI
The Case Files

Detective Blake promised the case files to Dave and Simon. And it was only a matter of time before they both came across something new about the case. It was confusing for Dave to digest that the Cooper family consulted Blake but didn't progress on the investigation. What was their reason? Did Blake know something more about the case? Is he hiding something about the Coopers? Such questions were rattling across Dave's mind.

On the other hand, Simon was on his phone. Dave grew suspicious of his friend's continuous cell phone activity. Was he hiding something from him?

They walked to their apartment after meeting Blake. He was in touch with them through messages, and it will take him some time to return to them.

Luckily, Aadi texted Dave back about the location of the Cooper family. He was able to locate them through his sources. His message read: "741B, Avenue Street, Silver Lake Town."

"I just received the location of the Cooper family from Aadi."

"Nice job, it means that they are still there." Simon was glad to hear about the update. "So, what do we know? Are we going to visit them?"

"No, not right now. Let's get those files from Blake first. Then we'll decide our next move. Till then, we should keep low and do our own research."

"Alright. Let's wait then." Simon sounded low.

The two friends agreed and started independently researching the different sources. Blake might take a lot of time to get back to them. Dave began investigating the online resources he had been working on before Simon's arrival. Meanwhile, his friend was busy using his mobile phone as usual. However, Dave didn't want to intervene with his friend immediately. He was waiting for the right time to look into his phone.

The day passed, Dave was restless, and Simon was on his third nap. He had nothing going on in his mind. It was almost evening, and Simon was already scrolling through the dinner options. But then the doorbell rang. He stood up and opened the door. It was none other than Detective Blake. He was wearing a long coat, which indicated the cold weather outside. He was holding a brown briefcase in his right hand.

"Come in Mr Blake?" Simon closed the door behind. "Take a seat."

Dave came from his room as well. "Detective, did you get it?"

"Yes, it's right here in my briefcase." He opened it and handed a photocopied version of Ella Cooper's missing case file. As expected, it was not a significant document, considering the tiny longevity of the investigation. Nonetheless, it was better than nothing, and Dave was looking forward to going into the details.

"You think you can work on this case by yourself?" Blake asked after handing the file to Dave. "I mean, you're an artist, what expertise do you have on crime and law?"

"It's a fair question. I can make you believe what I've been going through." Dave replied, agreeing with Blake's assumption.

"Could you elaborate? I know you were friends with the missing girl. But it's almost a year since she disappeared. I mean why are you looking into this right now?"

"Detective Blake." Dave took a seat. "I was okay and going on with my life, but a few days back, I saw Ella. At first, I thought it was just a misunderstanding or hallucination. But I saw her again last night."

"Are you serious?" The detective was dismayed.

"See." Dave was upset. "No one believes me." He looked at Simon. "Except for this idiot friend of mine." Simon was thinking about whether he was complimented or insulted.

Blake looked at Simon, staring at the two from the corner.

"You believe your friend?"

"A little bit but I am sure that there's something hidden in the case."

Blake nodded and looked back at Dave. "Listen guys, I have worked on plenty of cases myself and after all these years—I am in no position to not justify your reasons and motives." Blake pulled a cigarette from his coat. "Do you mind?"

"No, go on." He lit a cigarette, and now the entire apartment smelled like ashes. "However, I can say you need to work fast and smart because if someone is watching you, they expect you to make moves which they desire. And you don't want that?"

"Meaning?" Simon looked confused.

"It means that if Ella is alive, she's probably in danger and unsafe. Plus, it means that you guys could also be in danger."

"What do you mean by that?" Simon asked curiously.

"Oh you'll know when the time comes."

"So, what should we do next?" Dave asked in a serious tone.

Blake stood and lifted his bag. "Well, it's up to you. However, if you want my advice." He looked around and back at the two. "Stay out of this case. It's better for your life."

"Is that a threat?" Dave asked confusingly.

"No, consider it a good suggestion, or you might be in trouble. Goodbye, and try to keep this little chat between yourselves."

Blake left, leaving the two in confusion and distress.

"What the hell is wrong with that guy?" Simon spoke and broke the silence after the detective left.

"I don't know. Maybe too many cigarettes." Dave smiled as he opened the folder. "Let's get started."

He went to his room, leaving Simon to his own. He silently sat on the couch and went back to scrolling his phone. Dave read the case file, and there was almost no investigation. It was clear that someone didn't want to continue the process of finding Ella. All the leads include a bunch of statements from the people.

Dave's own statement was even included in the reports. Apart from that, everything was new but simultaneously pretty upsetting or disappointing for him. He read the entire thing in thirty minutes and couldn't find anything.

The investigation lasted three months. Only a few actions were taken during that period, which didn't lead anywhere. Dave was dissatisfied with the files but decided to give it another shot. He was paranoid—maybe he left something unread in those texts. However, Simon came to check on his friend.

"Hey, did you find anything?" He asked apathetically.

"Nah, but I am looking at this folder once again."

Simon nodded. "Alright. Would you like some coffee?"

"Sure." Dave replied.

"Alright, then the kitchen is all yours." Simon said sarcastically. "I don't know how to make one?"

"Are you serious?" Dave looked at his friend disappointingly. "You don't know such basic things. What will happen to you when the apocalypse comes?"

"If coffee is my priority in apocalyptic situations then it's already here."

Dave smiled deploringly. "You fool. Here, take these files. I'll make some coffee. Maybe you should also take a look at these reports."

"Alright, my friend."

Simon took Dave's files and sat down to read them. He was surprised to see the size of the small document. He started going through the file. Simon was a quick reader thanks to his years of experience reading novels.

Dave came back after five minutes with two cups of coffee.

"So, did you find anything remotely interesting?" Dave handed his friend a cup of coffee.

"Nah, I am just going through this, but I see something here. Did you find this suspicious as well?"

"What are you talking about?" Dave stood by his side to get a closer look.

"This name? Gary Wise? Do you know him?"

Dave took the file from his friend. "My God, how could I have missed this!"

"Because you are restless and impatient." Simon replied sarcastically.

"Very funny." Dave continued. "Who is he? I have never heard of this name before?"

"Well, there is his statement in the report. Supposedly, he was one of Ella's associates. Maybe relatives? What do you think?"

"It could be but I should have known about him from Ella. I mean she told me everything."

"Well, that was when you were together. She might have a personal space as well. Don't you think so?"

"Maybe you're right. I mean, we didn't talk much after winter break. We saw each other but things were never the same."

"Dave, I don't want to cross any line but what happened to you guys?" He continued even though Dave did not appreciate his intervention. "You were together for two years and all of a sudden you two broke up."

Dave took a deep breath. "It's a bit complicated but I'll tell you some other day. Let's focus on this Gary guy. What do you reckon?"

"I get it, you don't want to talk about your past but this thing that we're doing here is the past—your and mine. And I think I should know what we are doing here? I mean you're clearly hiding something."

Simon stood solid in his stance.

"Oh come on, don't act like you're not doing the same." Dave replied furiously.

Simon was stunned by the remark. "What do you mean?"

"You're on your phone all the time. Tell me, is it my parents who have asked you to keep an eye on me?"

"So what? They are your parents—they have the right to know that you're not losing your senses! I mean, did you really think that people would buy your whole baloney story?

"Don't you dare say that? I know I am fine and you're welcome to leave if you feel otherwise."

"It's not what I feel? I just want to help you so that you can close this ridiculous phase of your freaking life. You had everything going well when you were in the city. And being oblivious, you threw everything out of the window just to return here—a place that only gave you misery."

Dave was speechless. Simon left the room to pack his bag. He had enough of Dave's melodramatic adventure and was now willing to leave his friend behind. However, after a few minutes, Dave came out of the hall. "Let's go."

"Excuse me!"

"Come on, I have to show you something?"

"What is it?"

"Please don't ask any questions and come with me?"

Simon thought momentarily and looked at his friend, who seemed dead serious. "Alright, whatever it is? I'll be leaving once I come back."

The two left the apartment and were out on the streets. Dave took Simon to his old spot where he had gone the previous day. It was far from their place, but Simon didn't ask any questions. He didn't want to indulge in a short conversation with Dave. However, in the midway, Simon realised where they were going? After reaching the place, both sigh with relief as they gaze at the small, well-lit town.

"Why have you brought me here?"

"I was standing right here the other day," Dave said, looking across the road. "Ella stood there. She was real. I tried to reach her, but I couldn't." He took a deep breath. "It was the same place where we broke up. I remember that day as if it was yesterday. She called me to meet her. I missed my evening class to get here. I saw her; she was the most beautiful woman I have ever seen. However, I didn't expect that she wanted to move on." Dave was teary while Simon was listening with attention. "She just left after saying: it's over, I am sorry." He tried to control his emotions. "Two words sufficient to break anyone's heart. I was so confused and devastated that I didn't mumble or ask anything back. Somehow, I gathered my spirits to go back to my room. To this day, I haven't asked her why she broke up with me. And after she went missing, to be fair, I thought more about our relationship than her."

Dave was sat on the bench, broken and upset. "I don't know if she is alive or just exists in my mind. I just can't let her go. I want to know the truth—buried in the lies."

Simon took a seat by his friend. "It's alright, Dave. We'll find out the truth." He calmed the man. "Look at me." He gave Dave some confidence and offered his hand. "Together."

"Yes, together." They both shook hands.

"Thanks for letting me know. I know that you had something deep inside. Because you were never the same after Ella went missing. I mean, even before that, you changed a lot."

"It took me a lot of effort to put on a fake mask and pass those months, being around her."

"Well, you did a fine job. I must give you credit for that." Simon laughed. "Hiding all this pain takes a toll on everyone. But now it's all in the past and there is nothing you can do to change it. So, now all we have is a name. And I am asking you? What do you want to do with it?"

"Hmm, Gary Wise? Who is this guy?" Dave came back to his senses. "I think we should give him a visit."

"Alright. Let's find him." Simon took out the file from his coat.

"Wait, did you bring the file with you? Dave was surprised by his friend."

"I thought we might need it."

"Good thinking." Dave shook his head.

Simon navigated to Gary Wise on the report. According to that information, he is a 45-year-old doctor in Silver Lake Town. His official address was #081, Light Street, Silver Lake.

"Do you think that it's a coincidence that both Cooper family and this guy Gary Wise are in Silver Lake."

"I think he's their associate or something." Dave replied. "But yes, it's weird that the Cooper family had any sort of links in Silver Lake. Maybe we need to go there for some more information."

"We both can leave tomorrow morning." Simon suggested.

"Sounds like a plan?"

They both went back to town for some dinner. It was already late to book a train to Silver Lake. So, they decided to rent a car to the town. They packed their stuff for the brief stay in the nearby town.

"Are you planning to meet Aadi as well?" Simon asked as he finally shut down his small bag.

"Maybe, if he's available. I don't know what he is doing nowadays."

"And what about the Cooper family? Are we going to visit them?"

"It totally depends on the information which we get from Gary Wise. I mean, I am pretty pessimistic when it comes to planning. Nevertheless, let's see what happens next?"

They both decided to leave early in the morning since Silver Lake was around 100 miles from Pinewood. Also, their rental car needed some gas in the morning. Simon said good night to his friend. However, Dave was sleepless as he was still wondering about the case and thinking about the situation. He was glad to have Simon with him but knew it was detrimental to keep his friend alongside if things were to go sideways.

He hated this decision, but it was better for him to leave him behind. So, he decided to leave Pinewood in the middle of the night. He already had the keys to the car, which was parked below the rental office. All he needed to do was to wait for midnight, grab his stuff and leave for Silver Lake Town. It might take him four to five hours to reach the place. The full moon glimpsed across Pinewood—it was a sign for Dave to bid farewell to his sleepy friend. He took his bag on his shoulders and silently left the apartment.

VII
New Horizons

After driving for six hours, Dave was finally in Silver Lake Town. It was a beautiful place with many green trees and vibrant flowers. However, he was a little early, and there was still time for the sun to showcase everything with its light.

Dave stopped at scenic Silver Lake in the middle of town with nothing to do. He parked his car and stood by the lake. Some people were taking their morning walks there. The drive was not easy for Dave because of the unfamiliarity of the road.

Nonetheless, he was at the place, and now all he had to do was wait. He found a small step beside the large river body and sat there. Little did he know the time had passed, and now it was almost nine in the morning. The sun brought Dave back to his senses from all his daydreaming. He calmly picked up his coat and checked out his cell phone. There were several missed calls from Simon. However, it was not the time or place for him to explain everything that had happened the previous night.

After blocking his friend, Dave went to the car. He was able to locate Light Street in Silver Lake Town. However, it took him some manual effort to find the #081 house. Upon reaching the place, he parked his car and, through a small garden, stood against the front door. He knocked on the door a couple of times before it was answered. Surprisingly, it was a little girl that opened the door. She wore a frock that looked like a uniform. Before her, a lady came with a handbag on her side.

"Good morning, ma'am." Dave greeted the lady, who seemed to be in a little hurry. She wore a grey lady suit as if she were also leaving for work. She had long dark hair, a broad smile, and sharp facial features.

"Are you looking for someone?" She asked. "Macy! Go back inside and get ready for school. You'll be late."

"Yes, is this Gary Wise's house?"

"It is." She replied. "Unfortunately, he's not at home. Do you have an appointment?"

"No, I just wanted to see him."

"Well, in that case, you should visit him at the hospital. He's working an early shift there."

"The local hospital?"

"Yes," she replied but grew suspicious of Dave. "You're not local, are you?"

"No, actually I drove all the way from Pinewood to meet him."

"Pinewood? That's pretty far." She was astonished. "Is everything alright?"

Dave was hesitant to continue the conversation but had no other option. "Yes, everything is fine. It's just that I am here to consult him on behalf of my sick family member. I just want his opinion on the health situation. That's all."

"I see. Well, as I said earlier, he's at the hospital. Maybe I can give him a call so that you don't have to make an appointment."

"That'd be great. Thank you." Dave with a fake broad smile.

"Well, it's the least I can do. You drove all this way to meet him. It's the least we can do." The lady smiled and grabbed her phone from the purse.

"Your good name?" She asked.

"I am Dave."

"Nice to meet you, Dave. I am Kathy, Gary's wife." They both shook hands.

Kathy called Gary to give him information about Dave, who was patiently waiting to leave the house's porch.

After the call, Kathy looked at Dave with a broad smile. "Well, he's free and you can directly go to his office."

"Thank you so much Cathy, I appreciate it."

"Don't worry, do you want some tea or coffee?"

"No, no, I should get going as I have other places to be. Maybe some other day."

"Alright, have a good day."

"You, too, have a good one." Kathy closed the door, and Dave immediately rushed to his car. He drove to the hospital and eventually reached Gary's cabin. Apparently, Gary was a medicine specialist. Dave stood in front of the door and knocked three times. A man with a deep voice asked him to get inside.

"Hello, Dr Gary, I am Dave. You might be expecting me."

Dr Gary stood from his seat. He was a short guy with a dense beard, thin hair, a pointy face, and brown eyes. He was wearing a white coat over his jacket. "Hey, how are you doing?" They both shook hands. "Please, have a seat." Dave sat across from the doctor.

"So, Kathy told me you wanted to see me regarding some family emergency?" Gary asked as they opened a small register in front of him. He had a habit of taking notes during meetings with patients.

"Yes, it's the reason I told your wife but there is something else." Dave continued. "I am here to investigate the case of missing Ella Cooper."

Gary was flabbergasted. "Wait a minute, who the hell are you?" He was about to call security through the phone in front of his desk.

"Don't worry, I am not here to cause trouble. I just want some answers."

"I am not obliged to say anything to you. I mean, you're not a policeman, are you?" Gary asked formally.

"I know, but I want your help. I have seen the police records. In fact, I found out about you from one of your statements in the reports. I know you knew the Cooper family. So, just tell me if you know something about Ella?"

"What if I don't cooperate with you?"

Dave chucked a bit. "Then it will only be a matter of time before I can get some dirt on you and put you in jail."

"What the hell are you talking about?"

"Don't get me started. It will take me less than 24 hours to change your life for the worse."

"Are you threatening me?" Gary said in a nervous tone. And it was sufficient for Dave to realise that maybe the doctor was not so fair and righteous.

"Look, I am here for information. So, just give me what you have on Ella or her family, and I'll be on my way. I won't cause any trouble, I promise."

The doctor thought for a second. He didn't know Dave, but soon, he agreed to cooperate with the strange man.

"Alright but you have to believe in my word." The doctor sighed.

Dave nodded. "I am listening."

"Listen, everything I am about to share remains in these four walls. Can you promise me that?"

"It depends." Dave paused for a bit. "What will your next words be?"

"Alright. So it all started one day when I received a call from Mr Cooper—Ella's father."

"I know him."

Gary continued. "He asked me to visit him one early morning. I was working in Pinewood at the time. It was a few months before Ella disappeared. I reached their home, and it was Ella. She was pretty sick."

Dave was observant since he had never heard of Ella being sick before. However, he tried to hide his sentiments to be more stern.

"Really? What happened to her?"

"I don't know. She was not well. I brought her to the hospital and did some diagnostics. After a couple of days, the reports came." Gary looked outside through the window.

"Doctor?" Dave shouted in a low voice. He looked at him. "What was it?"

"Well, she was suffering from a severe heart problem."

"What?" Dave couldn't believe his ears.

"Yes, she didn't have much time left."

Dave was shocked upon hearing the revelation. "I don't understand. I never heard of this."

"They tried to keep the news private since they were looking for transplants nationwide."

"So, did she get the transplant?" Dave asked curiously.

"The family tried reaching out to different hospitals, but there were many implications. Ella's body was prone to immune disorders. So, finding the ideal donor for her was difficult."

"How long did she have without the transplant?"

"It varied entirely upon her lifestyle but it was certain that her next heart failure would have been her last."

Dave realised that it was at the same time they broke up. Maybe this was why she sheltered herself from him. However, he returned from such premises to focus on the current conversation.

"And she disappeared without ever getting a transplant?"

"Yes, as per my knowledge."

"And what about the Cooper family? Why did she leave Pinewood? Is it because of Ella's disappearance?"

"I don't know about that?" Gary replied hurriedly. "I mean I knew that they were here but I don't know the reason!"

"Are you serious? How'd you know that they were here?" Dave pressed the question.

"I saw Mr Cooper one day at the local market."

"Oh really?" Dave remarked tauntingly. "You happened to run against him in the market. That's weird."

"Give me a break. I told you everything. Now, please leave before I make a scene out of this situation. I don't care why you're here, but that's it from my side." Gary tried to threaten Dave, who got up, left the cabin without causing any more trouble and exited the hospital.

He still could not digest the news about Ella, who hid all her problems from everyone for so long. She was good at hiding her feelings, but Dave did not expect this. Nonetheless, he was one step closer in his pursuit, and now it was time to meet his old associate, Aadi. He texted the man who was waiting for him at his home.

Dave drove to Aadi's place to find the man reading a newspaper on the porch. He was taking the day off because of Dave and welcomed his friend in pyjamas and a white shirt. His round face was covered with a black beard, trimmed to perfection. Meanwhile, his hair was messy, and his brown eyes indicated he was still half asleep.

"How are you doing Dave?" They shook hands and hugged one another.

"I am great. Just wanted to see you." Dave smiled a bit.

"I am glad you're here." Aadi gestured to him to take a seat on the chair outside. He sat adjacent to him. "So, what can I get you?"

"Nothing at the moment, thanks for asking." There was a moment of silence.

"So, what brings you here?" Aadi started.

"Well, it's a long story but I am going to be straight with you. I am working on a case."

Aadi laughed. "You're joking, right?" He then looked at Dave, who was serious. "Oh, you're not joking! What case are you talking about?"

"You remember Ella?"

"Yes, your girlfriend from college. I heard about her. You were asking about her parents on the call."

"You're right." Dave continued. "I am working to find her."

Aadi thought for a second before opening his mouth, shocked. "Are you serious? Why? That's not your job."

"I know, and it wasn't something I planned to do, but how do I put this?" Dave tried his best to sound sane while explaining his encounter with Ella to Aadi.

"I saw Ella." He said straight up.

Dave told Aadi everything that had happened the days before, and Aadi's face was astonished and confused.

"Dave, let me ask you something?" Aadi said after hearing the incidents. "You're not intoxicated."

"Oh, come on, man. Don't give me this reply like everyone else."

"Thank god everybody else had the same reaction because if they didn't, I might question my own sanity."

"Please, Aadi be serious."

"Alright, Dave, I am just, you know, it's hard to wrap your mind upon hearing your story." He paused for a bit. "So, what's next for you? I mean, you already visited her doctor and know about her heart condition. Don't you think she's getting a transplant abroad in another country?"

"I mean, it's a possibility, but why hide? Or ran away from everything?" Dave sounded confused. "I don't know, but I need to get to the bottom of this."

"Well, I am here in case you need some help." Aadi assured his friend.

"Thanks, man, but I am working on this alone. I don't want anyone to get in trouble because of me."

"I understand that."

"So, where is uncle and aunt?"

"They are at work."

"Both of them?"

"Yes, why'd you ask this?"

"No, I thought maybe one of them was retired. I heard you say something about their retirement."

"Yes, my mother retired a few years ago but now she's working independently with an upcoming media business."

"That's nice."

"So there's usually no one in the house most of the time."

"I can see that." Dave paused for a bit. "Well, that's it for me, I must go."

"But wait, let's have some breakfast. What's so urgent?"

"I am going to see Ella's parents and confront them about the situation."

Aadi needed some clarification. "So, you're just going to tell them your whole story."

"Na, I'll just want to hear what they have to say?"

"And this conversation can't wait for a bit." Aadi persuaded his friend to stay for a while.

"I am sorry but I'll catch up with you later. Probably for a good cause."

Dave stood up and shook Aadi's hand to bid farewell for now. They both talked a bit about the case.

Dave mainly provided some details in case he needed additional information from Aadi. He entered his car and set himself up for the location of the Cooper family.

In the meantime, he checked his phone—there were some messages, but Simon had finally stopped calling him.

He reached the address given by the Aadi, which was comparatively small. Dave parked in front of the house and knocked on the door. Mr Cooper answered the door but was not surprised to see Dave.

"Hello, Dave, how are you?"

"Hello Mr Cooper." Dave greeted the man moderately.

"Come inside. I was expecting you." Mr Cooper closed the door.

"So, Dr Gary told me about you?"

"He happens to be my friend. You thought he wouldn't call me."

"Dave, it's so nice to see you." Mrs Cooper came and hugged him. "How are you doing?"

"I am doing good-." Dave couldn't even finish his sentence.

"Apart from causing ruckus in the morning." Mr Cooper said with frustration. "Take a seat."

"Let me bring something for you." Mrs. Cooper left to make breakfast for her guest. She was still naive to Dave's presence and sudden visit.

"Forgive me but I had no other option."

"Oh really, civility is the other option. Plus you didn't even think for a second that you may be crossing a line. He's my friend and a reputable man. How dare you threaten him like that?"

"See, I got carried away but I am looking for answers."

"Why? If I may ask?" Mr Cooper made a serious face. He fixed his eyes on Dave.

"Because I think I can find her." Dave replied confidently, making Mr Cooper intimidated.

"What do you mean by that? You're no police and all the investigation has been impractical."

Dave leaned a bit forward. "It's because you made it that way."

"What the hell are you trying to say?"

"I have seen the reports from the investigation and apart from a few statements—there was nothing going on in the case."

"Bullshit." Mr Cooper was pissed. "We tried our best and I was very strict on the officers. And to this day, I hope for some positive results. I even contacted a brilliant detective for the investigation."

"But then why'd you drop him off the case?"

"You know about him." Mr Cooper said with distress. "Never mind, he was costing us too much."

"I get it but where has all this led you?"

Mr Cooper was speechless as there was no comeback from such questioning.

"Alright. What do you want then and why are you here?"

"I just want to know why don't you tell us about Ella's health." Dave asked with a serious gaze.

"Because Ella didn't want you to know." He continued. "She loved you very much. And after her health revelation—she wanted to distance herself from the people she cared about."

Dave was getting emotional.

"I know you were together. And, yes, she broke up with you because of this. Because she didn't want to see you hurt."

"But Dr Gary told me that you guys were looking for donors."

"Yes, we were but the reality is there was no hope for her. And this makes me think, it's the reason why she left. So that I don't have to see her dead face."

Mr Cooper breathed a sigh of relief as if he had held the truth for so long in his mind. Dave didn't want to shed tears before Ella's parents, so he left the house. Mr Cooper didn't stop him, but neither questioned him further.

"Did he leave?" Mrs Cooper felt terrible when she came out as Dave left without saying goodbye. She was preparing tea for him in the kitchen while her husband sat there, lost in his thoughts.

Dave was moving towards his car without looking around, and suddenly, two men in uniforms appeared and forcefully escorted him to the police vehicle. At first, he tried to get free, but later, he realised he was getting arrested.

VIII
Compromised

"Can I make a call?" Dave asked as he stood in front of a tall police officer wearing black shades. The officer had a moustache and short hair trimmed on the sides.

"You can in some time, but before, I need to brief you on something," the officer said in a lazy tone.

"What do you mean by that?" Dave was confused.

"Officer Noch, bring him in." The officer ordered his subordinate to bring someone. It was none other than Dr. Gary. As soon as he walked in, Dave realised why he was there. He looked at Gary, who stood at his side with a little smirk on his face.

"Is this your guy?" The officer asked the distressed Gary Wise.

"Yes. officer. He's him."

"Alright then, take this vigilante in and show him our hospitality."

The police officer took Dave to the lockup; Dr Gary was not even hiding his smile anymore. It was not an ideal move on Dave's behalf to be a stud in an unfamiliar town. And the whole plan backfired on him. Nonetheless, now all he can do is wait for some external support.

Six hours passed, and Dave was still in custody. At first, he tried his best to confront the police officer, but soon he realised that there was no point in arguing with him. He was in no mood to make more enemies—so he just waited.

After ten hours, his friend, whom he had abandoned back at Pinewood, came to help. Simon, Aadi and a legal official joined them. Together, they helped Dave escape Gary Wise's charges. It took them another five to six hours to sort things out in the case.

Simon welcomed his friend with an infuriated face and a solemn tone.

"Wow, so you're a fugitive now." Simon taunted his friend right outside the police department.

"Simon, look, I am so sorry. But I had no other choice."

"Oh, please, you had another option to take me here with you. Now, you've successfully wasted our whole day." Aadi nodded as well. He did his best to keep a straight face in the situation.

"Listen, I had no idea that the doctor would call in an official."

"Well, if you hadn't threatened him then things would have been different."

Dave looked disappointed and tried to keep his mouth shut.

"Guys, as much as I like to be here and enjoy the drama. I need to go, I have some work to do in town. I'll catch up with you later if you're still around." Aadi interrupted and left after their lawyer.

"Sure, thanks Aadi and once again, thanks for the lawyer."

"Anytime." Aadi bid farewell to his friend outside the police department, and now it was Dave and Simon.

"So, what does it cost?" Dave asked, breaking the silence.

"Don't ask, you would have been in there longer if I didn't figure out what you did?"

"Fine, I get it. I messed up but don't continue with this matter." Dave cried aloud. "I don't care."

"You should care!" Simon shouted. "You're done."

"What do you mean?"

"You can't work on this case. It was one of the conditions in your bail. Any form of private investigation or vigilantism has to be prohibited by you. Plus, you can't talk to anyone remotely related to Dr Wise, and that includes Ella's parents."

"You're kidding me right."

Simon handed Dave some official papers. "I wish." He looked at the file and couldn't believe what he was seeing and hearing. "Dave, you're done my friend. No more playing Sherlock Holmes for you. Let's go back. We'll figure this out some other way."

Dave was speechless and devastated. He didn't say a word after sitting in the car as Simon was driving back to Pinewood.

"Dave, we'll find some other way."

"I don't know man." He broke the silence. "It's difficult to navigate through this situation." He continued. "Do you know about Ella's situation and her health?"

"Yes, Aadi told me. In fact, I even met her parents when I was bringing your car back here to the station." Dave looked at him shockingly. "Did you find anything uncommon or valuable?"

"Brother, I wasn't even thinking about the case when I met them; I just wanted to get you out of the custody."

"So thoughtful of you."

"Very funny," Simon replied in a harsh tone. "Listen, I made a promise to your parents that I would look after you, and that's the reason I came back looking for you."

Dave felt a bit guilty for leaving his friend behind. Simon was the only one who seemed to give a damn about his circumstances. Even though Aadi was a tremendous help, he didn't believe an ounce of the story that came out of Dave's consciousness.

"Let's go to Detective Blake." Dave replied to the original question.

"You mean after reaching Pinewood." Simon was not interested in that notion. However, he didn't contest the idea at that very moment. For him, it was crucial to take his friend away from the fuss of Silver Lake.

It was already midnight, and Dave was asleep in the car. Simon still had more than fifty kilometres to drive back to the town. They took a break before dinner, which was one reason Dave fell asleep.

They reached their apartment, and at that point, Dave sleepwalked to his room and fell on the bed. He had no idea of the journey and the route. Simon, too, was tired, and after assisting his friend, he went to sleep as well.

The morning came, and Dave was already ready to meet Blake. Simon saw him after he woke up. He was surprised but then remembered Dave's plan for the day. He didn't want Dave to discuss everything with Blake, so within five minutes, he got ready and dressed to meet the detective.

They went over to Blake, who was not surprised to see the two that early in the morning. He welcomed them to his apartment, where they took their seats. Detective Blake was also working on the case. He held a coffee mug in his right hand while the other was occupied with some sort of paper.

"What the hell are you both up to now?" The detective sat on a chair and put his cup on a mahogany table by his right side.

"Detective, we have a situation."

"What is it?"

Dave told everything that had happened the previous day, and Blake was not glad to hear anything.

"Well, I guess, the detective career is not for you." He chucked.

"Sir, this is not funny."

"Yes, it is. What do you reckon?" He looked at Simon. "Don't you think it's funny?"

Simon shrugged his shoulders, agreeing with Blake, and Dave couldn't believe his eyes. "You too."

"Sorry man, but last I checked, I was the one to set you free."

"Very supportive of you." Dave made an obnoxious impression.

Blake spoke in. "Hey, listen, I know that this case means something to you, and I wish I could help you, but I am occupied."

"With a case?" Simon asked.

"Yes." Blake replied. "So, its best for you to leave this all behind and go enjoy your life in the city. There's no point in bothering yourself with this crap."

"Man, got a point, Dave." Simon looked at Dave in hopes of departing from the case and town.

"Detective, may I ask about the case you're working on? I hope it's not confidential."

"No, in fact, I am glad you asked." He continued. "It's a murder case."

"In Pinewood." Simon intervened.

"Yes." Blake replied. He lighted a cigarette. "The man was 40."

"That's tragic," Dave said remorsefully. However, all of a sudden, an idea came to his mind.

"Detective, I have a proposition. Would you care to listen?" Dave said while Simon looked at him, knowing that something was fishy.

"Yes, go ahead."

"Can I help you in your case and afterwards would you care to return the favour?"

"Dave, I don't think he needs our help." Simon tried to stray the two away from the idea.

"I didn't ask you, Simon," Dave said irritatingly. "So, what do you think of Detective Blake?"

"Well, I could use some help in this case but I don't think you're capable. Plus, you might need some official licensing for private investigation."

"I guess, you can take me as your assistance—that way I can work without facing any legal troubles."

"That's a good idea but I have to report to the officials and I can't afford to keep you around them."

"Alright." Simon stood up. "Let's go, Dave."

"Woah, hold on for a second."

Dave sat back; meanwhile, Simon was pissed because of the entire conversation. He didn't like either of the ideas and couldn't wait to leave the town. However, his obligations made him susceptible to the whole scenario.

"We can start working from tomorrow." Blake broke the silence, and Dave's face lit up. "However, I only need one of you. I don't want too much of a crowd in my apartment.

"Very well." Simon left the place. Dave tried to stop him, but he didn't listen.

"You better get your friend," Blake said as he saw Simon leave disappointedly. "He seems like a good guy."

"Alright, I'll see you tomorrow."

Dave went after Simon, who was smoking a cigarette at Blake's entrance.

"Simon, I am so sorry but I have no other option."

"Are you out of your mind, Dave? I mean, what is wrong with you." He cried. "You are supposed to look at Ella's case. You did that. You failed miserably. And now you're proposing to work on another case for a detective you don't even know that well. What a joke?"

Dave couldn't say anything. Simon was right, but if Dave had been conducting his life logically, he should've never been here in the first place.

"Look, man, I don't know but my instincts say that Blake is our last option. I mean, we help him, and then he can help us. It's not a big deal."

"It's a big deal. You don't know what type of case he is working on? It's a murder, cruel people attached to such atrocious acts. You can be in danger. It's not a piece of cake for regular folks like us."

Simon was trying his best to change Dave's mind, but he knew that he might be wasting his time.

"I know that but I don't see this any other way. I have to do this." Dave paused and looked Simon right in the eyes. "With or without you."

"Alright then. I'll see you later." Simon threw his cigarette and went back into the streets. This time, Dave didn't say anything to stop him. He looked around and went the other way. There was still a whole day ahead of him. So, he tried to get some details about the case Blake was working on.

He went back to Blake's apartment, who was excited to see his partner.

"Welcome back." He said with a broad smile. "Where is your friend?"

"Umm, he's out for some fresh air."

"The guy deserves that. I mean, he seems like a good friend."

"He is, even though we both are quite often on different pages."

"I can see that." Blake said as he held a file in his hand. "So, why are you back?"

"Actually, I wanted to get some lead on the case. So that I can catch up with you tomorrow." Dave replied in a serious tone."

"That's very thoughtful of you." The detective complimented him and put some papers on a table in front of him. "Click some pictures. I don't make copies of the case I am working on."

Dave clicked some pictures for his investigation.

"Listen, kid. Don't mess this up. I am trusting you on this one. Make sure to keep all this to yourself. Am I clear,"

Dave nodded, put his phone back in his pocket and left. He dropped a message to Simon to come back to the apartment as he walked back. With some crucial information, Dave can get a headstart on Blake's case.

IX
The New Case

Simon was out of town the whole night. He didn't reply to any of Dave's texts or calls, which made Dave a little worried about his friend. However, he was busy as he read about the case that Blake was working on. Apparently, the guy who was killed was named Philip. He was a local store owner who was murdered in front of his own land. His death was due to a lethal blow to the back of the head, leaving him unconscious. His last known location was in the store when his younger brother saw him going for his home after his shift at the store. Later, he was found dead.

After getting into the details of the case, Dave decided to visit Blake. He might have been expecting him, and as far as Simon was concerned, he couldn't do much about him. He knew his way around, and that was the least of Dave's worries. After he got ready, he walked directly to Detective Blake's apartment. However, on the way, he sees Simon alongside Elliot. They both stood in front of him, and they seemed a bit drunk.

"So, the wannabe detective is on his way to work?" Simon said tauntingly.

"Look man, I am sorry but I had no other choice." Dave looked at Elliot. "Is he alright?"

"Again with the excuses." Simon continued. "I am trying my best to help you and all you do is betray me again and again."

"What else are you expecting from him?" Elliot intervened. "He's not good at promises."

"Elliot, shut up before I break your face." Dave got triggered by the remark.

"Oh, so now you're against us," Elliot said while being a little threatened. "Do you have any idea who you're working with? That Detective, he's a nobody—the man left his job. He's incompetent but to be fair, you deserve someone like him by your side."

Dave didn't say much and went his way. It was not the right time to face his friends.

"Go on, Mr Detective. Live your delusion." Simon shouted behind his back, and that was the last thing Dave heard before taking the right side at the end of the street. He was alone and free from his friends, and it was good for him. However, Elliot's remarks about Blake were troubling. Nonetheless, he had no other option but to work with the Detective.

He arrived at his place only to find that the man was still asleep. Also, he was not expecting him that early in the morning.

"Are you insomniac?" Blake asked as he was still in sleep.

"I thought we could start from today."

"I told you but that doesn't mean nine in the morning, my friend." Blake poured a glass of water. "But now that you're here. Let's get going." He smiled at him.

"I studied the files which I took home on my phone. It's a little tricky."

"How so?"

"I mean, there is not a lot of evidence that I can see or break through."

Blake was surprised since he didn't expect the rookie to study the basic details of the case. "Did you find anything else useful? I mean, where should we start from?"

"That's your call but we can do some background checks on the guy and later on meet with his close people."

"That's the hard part but you're not wrong. However, we need to be careful. I mean you're my responsibility and I don't want you to get hurt." Blake took his seat. "So, make sure to follow my lead. Am I clear?"

"Yes, right." Dave looked a bit confused. "Detective, I have some personal questions. Can I ask?"

"Shoot."

"Who is employing you for the case? Is it the man's family or any other personality?"

"Consider it as a favour I owe to one of my colleagues in the police station."

"So, you're not getting paid." Dave was surprised to hear about Blake's situation.

"For this case, but don't worry. I will charge you when I start working on the case of the missing girl. Blake took a cigarette from his side pocket. "What's her name again?"

"Ella." Dave replied, and Blake gestured to him to grab a seat at the table.

"Yes, I remember," Blake lit a cigarette while Dave sat on a chair adjacent to the table and started working on the documents. Blake was a very patient person. He was never in a hurry and always looked focused on the case, but he smoked continuously. The whole house smelled of burned papers and residues, and only an outsider could sense it.

On the other hand, Dave was on a different level when it comes to patience and working. He was looking to solve the case as soon as possible so that he could go back to finding Ella. So, using little time, he made a list of people associated with the case. First and foremost was the victim and his family. Other than that, there was not a lot of information on Philip's whereabouts. The case was two weeks old, and looking at the investigation, it had nothing apart from some basic reports.

Half an hour passed, and Blake came out of his room. He took a shower and changed into formal attire. The man was ready to go out and start working.

"Let's go Dave."

"Where are we going?" Dave was still working on his paperwork but was excited to see the man working.

"We are going to meet the man's brother. Jade."

"Alright?" Dave looked confused. "But you already have him on the reports."

"That's not mine. I landed a case a few days after the police investigation, and to be honest, this is technically the first day I am doing something on the case."

"Really? But the first time I came, I saw you working."

"That's a wrong assumption. I was playing chess on my phone." They both laughed it off. "Let's hurry up."

Both of them exited the apartment and sat in Blake's old car to visit Jade at their store. It was not far, but Blake wanted to avoid roaming through the streets.

"So, what are you looking for exactly to kickstart the case?" Dave asked his fellow companion.

Blake looked at him with a weird smirk on his face.

"What?"

"Dave, we don't kickstart the case, it's not a business."

"Can you elaborate?" Dave asked, being a novice. He wanted to know more about the Detective.

"We investigate the case and look for patterns which are interconnected. And once we have something which in some cases does not make any sense while in others makes the most, then we try that angle and see what comes next?"

"So, what do you think happened to Philip?" Dave continued. "Is this a feud or just an accident?"

"I can't say anything now but from what I've seen it could be something more."

"You mean, there is something else?"

"As I say, it could be anything?"

They both reached the store. It was a furniture store. Philip and his brother Jade collectively worked at the shop. It was a family-owned business passed on to them by their late father. Jade was dressed in formal attire and was eagerly waiting for the investigators. He was in his mid-30s, had average height, short hair, a clean-shaven face, and was groomed to perfection. Anyone can see the sadness in his eyes; he was going through a period of mourning, and Dave realised this as soon as he stepped out of the car. Again, it was Blake's case, so Dave tried to keep his distance during the conversation.

"Jade, thank you for talking with us."

"Detective, I'll do anything for your assistance." They all shook hands. "So, is there any progress in the investigation?" He continued with curiosity.

"Jade, I am working my best and sooner, I'll get to the bottom of the situation."

"I know, and no offence to you, our police department is horrid. They are a bunch of incapable people. Pardon my language, but they are good for nothing."

"None taken," Blake replied with a smile. "I don't work at the Police department, so I couldn't care less. They brought me in for the case as they needed more potency."

"And you're doing the same with this young officer." Jade looked at Dave with an encouraging gaze.

"Yes, this gent here has a sharp mind, and I am sure he will surprise us all." Dave tried his best to fake a smile the entire time, along with an intense face, depending on the tone of the conversation.

"So, let's get inside and we can have a word over a coffee."

Jade took the two inside his furniture store and made them sit at the reception. Considering the size of the town, it was a massive store.

"Who is buying all this stuff?" The thought came into Dave's mind.

"So, Jade tell me everything that happened?"

Jade was sitting across from the two investigators. He asked his worker to bring some coffee and snacks for the visitors.

"It was friday. I was on my way to the store. I received a call from Philip. He wanted to leave early as he was feeling a bit sick."

"Was it anything serious?" Blake enquired.

"No, it was just a migraine. He wanted a break for the rest of the day."

Blake took out a small diary and started writing a bunch of bullet points. Dave was intimidated and followed in his footsteps. However, he didn't have any pen or paper, so he decided to take notes on his cell phone. Blake saw this, but he chose not to focus on it.

Jade continued with his story and became a bit emotional. "It was the last time I saw him. He exited through that door to walk back home but he didn't reach."

"When did you become a little suspicious?"

"Well, after I closed the store and went to my apartment down the aisle, he wasn't returning my calls. I had some business to discuss with him. I took some dinner for him, but upon reaching his house, it was locked. I waited some time outside his place, but he didn't come. The next day, I learned about his demise."

"What about his family?"

"He has a wife and two kids but they are back in our hometown."

"Really, where are you guys from?"

"We are from Hilltown. Our father owned these chained furniture stores in various locations. So, we have to take care of them alternatingly."

"Wow, that's a lot of travelling business."

"Yes, it is. In fact, we have bought residential properties at different locations." Dave looked surprised as he didn't think that the Jade family was very wealthy.

"Why don't you live with your brother?" Blake asked as he rolled his page over.

"Because I have my own place here in the North end of the town by the old college. It is nearer to the store. I bought it a couple of years ago. Ever since I've been living there, whenever I am in town."

"And I suppose you're not married."

"No, I am not."

"Jade, can you tell me what happened next after you heard about your brother?"

"Well, the police asked me to come to the department. They told me that a local man found him on the side of the road opposite a public park. It was not far from Philip's house. But it was too late. Someone had knocked him out with a lethal blow, and he was no more."

"Alright. The reports say it was internal bleeding but as you know it was the cause of death. And I am looking for the real cause."

"I get it. But you have to work fast as those people might get away with such a horrendous crime."

"I'll assure you that I will get him. Do you know this guy Rick, the man who found your brother?"

"No, I don't." Jade replied.

Blake stood up. "Alright, thanks for your time." They shook hands, and Dave followed Blake outside.

"So, detective, where to now?"

"As I said earlier, let's give Rick a visit."

"Do you have his address?"

"I do." He looked confidently at his partner. "Let's go."

They both traveled to the residential area of Pinewood. According to the police reports, Rick lived in a community of local farmers. He himself owned some land in Pinewood, where he had his own farm. Upon reaching the place, they tried to find Rick, but to their surprise, the police were already present.

"Detective Blake." A voice shouted. It was one of the police officers at the scene. "How are you doing?"

"Officer Harris. What the hell are you doing here?" Blake was not happy to see him.

Office Harris was an old man of medium height with a bald head and a small moustache. He was one of the department's oldest officers.

"Actually, I have something for you."

"What do you mean?"

He laughed a bit. "I see you're working on a murder case. Well, let me add a missing case to the list."

"What?" Blake cried. "Who's missing?"

"Probably the man you have come to see."

"Oh crap." Blake was disappointed and frustrated.

Harris put his hand on his shoulder as a gesture. "Keep up the great work, kid." He smiled at Dave and left. At that moment, Dave realised he was putting himself into a rabbit hole of endless investigations and angles.

X

The Missing Link

After Rick's disappearance, the case became a lot more complicated than before. It was no coincidence that one of the critical persons in Philip's case was missing. Someone was a step ahead of Blake, and it clearly bothered him.

Blake didn't talk much after the new revelation. Dave was also stuck in the middle of nowhere. He wanted it all to end as soon as possible so that he could find Ella. However, the situation was going downhill. He needed help, so he called Simon to meet at a local pub.

Blake was back at his apartment, working on the case. He didn't need Dave to solve the case—it was more of a monetary reason, as he needed someone to finance his life. He was broke and had little money to fund his detective career.

Dave sat on a tall stool with a beer in his hand. Then he felt a sudden tap on his shoulder. It was Simon alongside Elliot. He didn't expect Elliot, but nonetheless, he welcomed his old pal.

"What is going on, our private detective?" Simon asked sarcastically, but after seeing Dave's despair, he decided not to tease him further.

"Hey, guys. How are you?" He shook their hands. "What's up Elliot?"

"Nothing, I heard you were offering some drinks so I joined Simon, in case he needs a ride back home."

"Well, that's thoughtful of you. Here, grab a seat."

They sat on Dave's left side. He ordered some drinks and snacks for them. Both of them were chilled, considering everything that happened a few days ago.

"Simon, I am sorry about what happened, but thanks for coming."

"It's ok, it's my fault, I overreacted a bit, but you're good." He took a sip. "So, what is going on?"

"Well, there's a bit of a hindrance in Blake's case."

"Hindrance?"

"Yes, the man who found the dead person is missing. And now, it's our job to find him as well."

Simon was astonished. "It looks like you're in for a long case."

"You're right." Elliot tried his best to participate in the conversation, but Dave decided not to indulge with him. He only tolerated him but didn't want to discuss the case, life or anything.

"So, what do you need?" Simon requested curiously.

"I want to know are you still here?"

"Here, in town?" He looked confused. "Yes, but only for a couple of days. I need to go back to the city for some work."

"Ok, right, sure," Dave replied in despair.

"What is it? Do you need something?"

"I just want to know if you can investigate Ella's case for the time when I am with Blake for his case."

"You're not serious?" Elliot said, interrupting the two. "What the hell is wrong with you? First, you lie to him and then you expect him to work for you. How low can you go?"

Dave was speechless, and he didn't want to argue with Elliot.

"Simon, I am just asking, you don't have to do this."

"I can do it for a week or two, but after that, I am going back and also expect the same from you." He offered his hand in good faith. Dave was glad to have Simon backing him up.

"I'll promise." Dave replied.

This was different from the sight that pleased Elliot. "Oh man, go to hell, both of you. You've lost your mind." He left the bar with his drink on the table.

"Let me get him back." Simon went after Elliot, and after a few minutes, both returned. Elliot was comparatively silent than before, and Dave decided not to say a word. However, Elliot sat on the far end of the pub to showcase his disapproval.

"Is he good?" Dave asked Simon, who was sitting on his side.

"He's good. Besides wishing to punch you in the face, he's alright."

They both smiled.

"Yup, I can't change that." Dave sighed and closed his eyes.

His phone had a notification. It was a message from the detective who wanted to see him urgently. Dave immediately finished his drink and went to Blake's apartment.

"I'll see you later." He bid farewell to Simon, who was still midway through his beer bottle.

"Alright. I'll see what I can get on Ella. Don't worry, I'll try my best."

Simon gently patted his shoulders, and the man disappeared in the middle of the night. Elliot saw all this from across the corner.

Upon reaching Blake's apartment, Dave was not surprised to see him working on the study. He asked him to take a seat.

"You wanted to see me?" Dave asked in a concerned tone.

"Yes, Dave, thanks for coming." He said to the rookie. "Listen, you want me to work on Ella's case. In return, you're helping me, but I must be clear and honest with you. I don't think I can help you with Ella's investigation."

Dave was shocked upon hearing this. "What do you mean? What's wrong?"

"It's just-I have a lot on my plate already with this murder and now the missing one. I don't know if I am available to help you. And it's very difficult for me to let you go since I am not getting paid in this particular investigation."

"Detective, I can understand but trust me I know you can do this. I am not going anywhere nor is my case. So, please focus on one case at a time."

"Dave, I don't know how long all this will go on? It's better for you to just consult someone else."

"Who do you think is going to help me after listening to my situation? You're the only insane one out here and the partial reason for that is the money. So, just hold on and see what you can do?"

"Alright, I just wanted to be honest about my situation. I don't want to seem like a guy hungry for money from an innocent guy like you."

"Great, thanks for being so transparent. Shall we start?"

"Yes, come here."

Dave went across the room and stood at the table. Blake wanted to show him something about Rick.

"I got some details about Rick and there is nothing about him in the local directories."

"It means that he's not a bad apple."

"You can say that but there has to be something about him in the public records."

"What about the police reports during Philip's investigation?"

"They only had his name, address and that's it."

"What about the lands and his position among local farmers?"

"It was a hoax, he probably used it to blend in with the others."

Dave was confused as hell. "He didn't own any land."

"Not that we know of!"

"So, you're saying that this guy can be the killer and used a witness card to escape the police."

"Yes, he could be. Plus, having zero information about him makes the situation a whole lot more complicated and puzzling."

"How can we find him?"

"Well, we need to enquire people around his address."

"Sure, who do you have in mind?"

"The representative of the community. His name is Wallace and he's one of the most trustworthy farmers out there. First thing tomorrow is we'll give him a visit and see what he has to say about this Rick guy."

"Alright. I'll meet you there." Dave was on his way out, but then he realised something. "Wait a sec. How does that police officer," Dave tried to remember the name. "Officer Harris knows about him? Is he working on the case as well?"

Blake replied. "It's complicated, but I'll let you know." Dave realised something was happening between the police and Blake but decided to let it go. It was night, and the streets of Pinewood were pretty lit. Dave didn't want to return to his apartment as he was not asleep. So, he decided to roam around the town and visit his old spot above the town. It was far, but he was steady and reached it. Upon reaching the place, he decided to sit and enjoy the city lights. He took a breath and two to reflect on the situation.

The last few days have been difficult for him, and he couldn't believe his situation. He closed his eyes and started contemplating the problem at hand. However, suddenly, he felt someone standing behind his back. He opened his eyes and looked at the lean, dark figure. It was Ella; she looked right into Dave's eyes. But this time, Dave didn't react in a hateful manner. He waited and didn't say a word. Ella elegantly moved in front of him and sat by his side. He couldn't believe his eyes, thinking he was in a dream. But what is a dream? And what is the truth? Dave had no idea at the moment.

"Are you real?" The first question came out of Dave's mouth. He couldn't speak clearly.

"What do you think?" She said in a mild tone.

"I don't even know what's real?" Dave replied as he was watching Ella without blinking his eyes. "What do you want? Why are you here?"

"Justice." She replied menacingly. "You didn't come to save me." She had an angry facial expression.

"What do you mean?" Dave wanted to move but couldn't, and suddenly, he blinked, and she was gone. Maybe it was a dream, and everything was an illusion inside Dave's mind. The encounter caused a sudden pain in Dave's head, and he decided to return to his place. Everything was getting intricate, and he wanted to escape Pinewood before losing his sanity.

After reaching his apartment, he found that it was open. Dave clearly remembered that he had locked it. Maybe Simon was sleeping in. He looked around the flat but couldn't find his friend. It was a pretty odd situation. However, his head was exploding, so he took an analgesic to calm his body. He rested on a sofa and fell asleep.

The morning came, and he was still nauseous; he looked around and saw someone in his periphery. It was frightening initially, but he realised it was only Simon.

"Hey man, do you need some coffee?" Simon offered Dave a big mug of black coffee.

"When did you come?"

"Last night." He replied as he stirred some coffee in a white mug.

"Really, because the door was opened, though I couldn't find you in the apartment."

"Are you kidding? I was in my room. Maybe you were tired because you were asleep on the couch when I heard the door open."

"Maybe you're right."

Dave didn't pay much attention to the situation. He was fatigued, but then he remembered that he needed to be at Blake's as soon as possible. He immediately stood from the couch and went in to take a shower. Simon was roaming around the apartment, whisking the coffee.

After Dave had freshened up, he sat with Simon, who had trouble getting some details about Ella.

"So, where are you going today?" Simon asked as he offered some coffee to Dave, who was trying his best to dry his soaked hair.

"Well, we have a name and now we need to look into it."

"Oh yeah? What else is going on?"

"Nothing." Dave shrugged his shoulders. "It's only been a couple of days."

"I know." Simon gasped. "I am also completely clueless on Ella." Dave looked at him curiously. "We need to find something out of thin air. That is the only way to get behind all this mess."

"You're right but it's not as easy as it looks."

"Sure."

Dave left for Wallace's place, where Blake was supposed to meet him. He messaged the detective before leaving. He was surprised to see Blake reach the place before him, considering his time management—he was standing with the man, and they were chatting. Wallace was a short man with a white beard, wearing a muffler and a winter cap. He was around 60 and seemed like one of the old professors at the college.

"Dave, glad you're here. Meet Mr Wallace." He shook his hand. "He's one of the biggest local farmers of Pinewood."

"Nice to meet you, sir, and thanks for the fresh vegetables." Dave tried his best to make a good impression on Mr Wallace.

Wallace gave a big smile even though he seemed stiff and strict. "Police branches are desperate to recruit officers at such a young age." He remarked as he looked at Dave.

"You're right, but he's not as young as you think." Blake stepped into the conversation before Dave said something unfit for the case. "So, as we were talking, what do you know about Rick?"

"Well, he's a fake. There is no one named Rick in this area or our community. I know everyone in this locality." He coughed and continued. "Look, I am getting old and sometimes I forget things but I sure made to look into the papers of the society and there was no one named Rick."

"Alright." Blake assured the man he trusted his word. "How many people live in your community?"

"Over three thousand I guess but it's a fluctuating number."

"I can see that since there's an on and off season in your job."

"Yeah, you get it."

"Look Mr Wallace, I'll be quite frank with you, this Rick guy is the only thing we have on the murder case. So, I'll be grateful if you can give me anything about him."

"I will try my best Detective."

Blake nodded in agreement and was on his way to his car. Dave was right by him, and then, suddenly, he looked at a tiny camera on the roadside solar light.

"Wait a minute, will you?" He went back to Wallace. Dave wanted to go but saw from a distance. They talked for a bit before shaking each other's hands. Blake handed him a small piece of paper, which seemed like a small card. He went back to his car.

"What happened? Did you forget something?"

"No, I handed him a photograph of Rick and asked him to check those cameras." He pointed to the surveillance.

"Oh great. Maybe we can find something on the tape." Dave said enthusiastically. "But don't you think we have seen those tapes in front of him. What if this Wallace guy plays smart?"

"I don't think he will because he's a reputed guy. Plus, I don't want to push their boundaries as long as they are cooperating."

"They can send us a few steps back on the investigation," Dave replied confidently.

"Hmmm, maybe you're right. Alright then, you go with him, look through those cameras, and find this guy. Think you can do that?" Blake asked sincerely of Dave.

"Sure. I'll catch up with you later."

Dave went to Wallace to trace Rick in the surveillance. If he had ever been in the town, there was a chance he would have been in the village as he knew about the place and the community. After putting Dave to the task, Blake went back to the town. He wanted to see Jade once again regarding the case. He went into the store but was surprised to find a different reception. Apparently, Jade was out of town for some business work. He tried to call his phone, but it was busy. So, Blake told the lady at the store to reach him once her boss was in town.

The signs did not look promising for Jade, and Blake grew suspicious of his activity. Plus, moving out of town only after a few days of losing a family member is never a good impression. Without much at hand, Blake's only hope was to find something on those cameras. He was in touch with Dave through the cell phone, and after a whole pack of cigarettes and an afternoon, Dave had some news.

Blake immediately reached Wallace's place and was excited to see Dave's smile alongside Wallace.

"I have something good on my hands?"

"What is it?" Blake asked curiously.

He showed him a photograph, which he had taken from the tape. It was Rick standing with a man from the farmer's community. His name was Kyle, and Wallace knew him.

XI

Camaraderie

Kyle had lived in Pinewood for over twenty years. He left his hometown after investing most of his ancestral money in buying land. He had a great farm and a local shop where he used to sell his products. He was one of the most trustworthy and loyal people Wallace knew in his community. Wallace was wholly devastated upon seeing Kyle with the potential suspect.

Wallace led Blake and Dave to Kyle's place. He was unmarried and had drinking problems, but this was not comprehensible. Wallace tried his best to back Kyle with his words and positive opinions. Still, none of them mattered to the investigators.

"Wallace, I think you should let us talk to him privately. If something comes up, I'll get back to you." Blake immediately removed Wallace from being active in the investigation even though he was helping them a lot.

"Alright detective but please don't be hard on him. He's going through some tough times."

"You mean his addiction?" Dave asked as they talked about the man previously.

"Yes, the drinking problem."

Blake looked at Wallace. "Don't worry, sir, I'll just have a word with him."

They were standing outside, looking around. It was a small place with two windows on each side of the front door. Blake knocked at the door. However, there was no response from the inside. He decided to wait for some time before trying other ways to reach the man.

"Mr Kyle! Are you in there?" Dave shouted from the window.

"What the hell are you doing?" Blake was pissed at him for making nonsensical noise. However, it worked for him as someone heard him from the inside.

A middle-aged man in a white vest and blue jeans opened the door. He had messy hair, an ungroomed beard, and grey hair, and his odour spoke volumes about the alcohol from the previous night.

"Yes, can I help you?"

"Hello, sorry to disturb you at this time of the day but we're looking for Mr Kyle."

"You're speaking to him." The man looked confused. "What do you need?"

"Actually I am Detective Blake and I am here to investigate the murder case of the local store owner. Have you heard about that case?"

Kyle was alert and clear in this speech. "Yes, the person was found dead."

"Well, I am here to ask you about a man." Blake took out the photograph.

"I don't think I can help you but sure, show me the photograph."

Blake showed him the photo of the suspect with Kyle.

"Are you kidding me ?" Kyle was shocked as he mumbled something in his mouth. "He's Rick. But where did you find this photograph?"

"That's the least of your worries," Blake replied. "Do you know where he is?" He put the photo back in his pocket. Kyle came out of the house and closed the door behind him.

"He's one of my workers." He looked confused. "However, he's out of town."

"How'd you know that?"

"Well, he texted me that he had an urgent piece of work out of town. So, he'll not be available for work for some time."

Blake looked at Dave, listening to the conversation carefully and evaluating everything that came out of Kyle's mouth.

"How long was he working with you?"

"Well not that long. I mean, he came probably three months back. I don't know exactly but he seemed like a nice guy."

"He might be but he was the first person who saw Philip dead. And it's possible that he's behind all this and now he's missing."

"What else do you know about him?" Blake took a small diary from his back pocket to note some new details.

Kyle tried his best to think of something but was not thinking correctly. Having two anonymous people at your door in the middle of the day asking for a murder case is a stretch for anyone. "Look, detective, I don't know what to say right now, but there's one thing I can tell you about Rick." He paused for a second. "He's very pleasant, and I don't think he's your man."

Blake chucked. "I am not saying that but you never know with these unknown guys coming into town for work. They are pretty good at bluffing. You know what I mean?"

"I get that but seriously I don't have anything on the guy but if he'll return I'll be the first one to inform you."

"I am sure you'll do that but I don't think he's returning anytime soon so just think it through. There has to be something."

"Alright, but give me a minute. Would you mind if I went inside? You can also sit instead of standing in the pungent sunlight."

"That'd be great." All three of them went inside. Blake and Dave sit on the couch while Kyle goes to his room to get some details about Rick. The place smelled of alcohol, and it was clear from the mess that they were at the home of a very unstable man.

"Do you think he knows where he is?" Dave said as they took a look around.

"I don't know, I mean, look at this place; it's a shithole with piles of crap." Blake was disgusted by the place. "This guy is giving me a run for my money when it comes to unhealthy living."

"Right. Take the alcoholic scent away from this place, and I couldn't differentiate between this and your apartment." Dave laughed it off.

Kyle came out of his room with some papers. He sat before them and handed the sheets to the detective, who opened the folds. He took the papers and saw some details about Rick.

"It's mandatory for us to have some sort of background information on the people we hire for work."

"Yes, but I don't think it's true. Did you do some background check on this?" Asked Blake as he was going through the information.

"No, I don't."

"Then I don't think it's useful for us but nevertheless I'll keep it."

Blake stood from his seat. "Let us know if you have anything else on Rick."

Kyle was in tension. "Wait. I have something else." He took out his phone and showed them a number. "I don't know, but a couple of weeks back, someone called on my cell asking for Rick."

"Really! What does he say?"

"Nothing, it was a man asking for Rick. I don't know how he got my number but it was a bit weird."

"Did he say anything else?"

"Nah, he sounded frustrated and hung up the phone after a few seconds."

"Can you note this number for me, my cell is dead." Blake instructed and handed the phone to Dave, who immediately saved the number in his cell.

"Thanks, Kyle. It might be a great lead for us." After returning the phone, they left the place, searching for the new number. Someone might have blown Rick's cover, and now it was only a matter of time before they visited the anonymous guy.

"Detective, can we trace this?" I asked Dave, who also sent the number to Blake's cell.

"Yes, but we need some assistance for that." He sighed. "I mean it's not easy to get the service providers to locate a cell phone without a warrant."

"So what do we do now?" Dave said despairingly.

"Don't worry, I have some connections which will sort this all out. Did you send me the number?"

"Yes. It's in your cell."

"Good, let me visit one of my associates. In the meantime, can you go and do some investigation regarding

Kyle. I mean, it's a possibility that he's screwing us."

"Yeah, you have a point. The man seemed as if he was hiding something. I couldn't help noticing."

"Yup. So, I'll call you once I have the details on the number."

"Great." Dave left in a positive spirit.

Blake drove away, and Dave was alone. However, he didn't intend to look after Kyle's angle. He received a call from Simon, who wanted to see him regarding Ella. Without wasting much time, he took a ride back to his apartment.

As he entered the building, he saw Simon resting on the couch.

"What is it?"

"Thank God you're here." Simon stood up. "Come take a look at this."

Simon showed Dave's picture in a newspaper article titled 'A young man threatens the local doctor.' Gary Wise with a big statement.

"Where'd you get this?"

"Aadi sent me. He thought you might get furious so he sent me instead."

"Well, I am not furious but I am a little pissed."

"Why is this doctor against you so much?"

"I don't know and I don't care. Leave him and let it be. He can't do anything to me so that's that."

"Alright. My bad."

Dave took a deep breath and relaxed on the couch. "What else do you have?"

"Nothing, I thought you wanted to know about this."

"Thanks for keeping me posted but it's not something I need to know in the future."

"Ok, got it." Simon took his phone. "So, what is going on with you?"

"Nothing, I had to do something but then I saw your message and came right here." Dave was constantly looking at his cell. "The detective is working on something while I am here."

"Alright, make yourself at home and I'll work on my thing."

"Sure."

Dave lay on his back to take a nap but was asleep for the entire afternoon. The sun was setting, and the detective still had no reply. He sent a message from his cell to Blake, but there was no reply. After waiting for a few minutes, he went back to sleep.

The evening unfolded, and Simon tried to wake Dave from his sleep. At the same time, Blake called. Dave hurriedly woke up and was out of the apartment. Apparently, Blake was waiting for him down the street. He went to his car and sat in the passenger seat. Blake was smoking and on a call.

"Hey, you good?" Dave asked as he put his coat on the back seat.

"Yes, I am good." Blake threw the cigarette out of the window. "We need to go. Are you ready?"

"Where?"

"Ivory town."

"What, wait, why?" Dave looked confused. "That's my home town."

Blake couldn't believe this. "Really, well, that's interesting."

"What do you mean?"

"Look, the name of the caller is Henry, he's a local electrician in Ivory town, I have other details about him as well. He's our guy."

"That's great but is it necessary for me to go with you?" Dave asked diplomatically, as he didn't want to see any familiar faces in his town.

"Dave, don't worry, no one will know that you were there." He paused to give some time for Dave to think this through. "We'll go and have a chat with Henry and then return. Plus, it's already late and no one will expect you at night."

Dave thought for a bit and agreed to the trip. "Let's go then."

"Do you want to grab something from the apartment?"

"No, I am fine."

"Good, we'll grab something for Dinner on the road."

"Sounds good to me."

Both left for Ivory Town in the evening. Dave conveyed his plan to Simon through the cell phone. The place was a few hours from Pinewood, and they needed to take some breaks. However, they were scheduled to reach the town before midnight.

XII

Home Town

It's been over eight months since Dave was in his hometown. So, it was a little tricky for him to visit his place without informing any of his family members. But it was how things were supposed to be; plus, he didn't want anyone to make assumptions about his whereabouts, as only a few people thought Dave was rational.

"So, you grew up here?" Blake asked as they entered the location.

"Yes, I did, in fact. I nearly lived my whole life in Ivory town." Dave took a deep breath.

"Well, I have been here before." Dave looked at Blake with a questionable expression. "Yes, it was a case a couple of years back. My boss and I stayed here for a few weeks to investigate a case."

"Really? It was when you were still associated with the police department."

"Yes."

"Look, detective, I don't want to make any assumptions but what is with you and the police?" Blake raised his eyebrows in a baffling manner. "I am sorry but why are you working for them? You obviously resigned from your position."

"Yes, I was free but something came up and it's more of a promise to an old friend."

"What's in it for you?"

"Nothing is just a mere responsibility. But leave it. Let's focus on the work."

Blake was hesitant to speak further about his past. He had his own problems, and Dave wanted to know more about his associate.

"We're almost here?" Blake stopped in front of a shady house. The place was dark, and it seemed no one was home or asleep. It was almost midnight, and there was no place for the two to go. They were stuck in the middle of two possible scenarios.

Dave exited his car to take a deep stretch, and Blake was still in. He pulled a cigarette from his coat. It had been a long and persistent drive. "What should we do?"

"Well, let's see if someone's home."

"Really!." Dave said defensively. "I will not go to a stranger's house and knock in the middle of the night. I might get shot or stabbed! Who knows?"

"Then I think we have to wait, but we don't have a place to rest. What do you think we should do then? Freeze here in the car," Blake said displeasedly.

"I can rent a motel if you like but they are on the east side of the town."

"Nah man, I don't want to miss this opportunity." Blake continued. "Our guy is in there and this is our chance."

The two of them were arguing back and forth, making their points. However, they didn't realise that their little street debate had caught someone's attention.

"Is there a problem?" A voice came from one of the houses, and a man stood on the street beneath a yellow light bulb. Both of them were caught in the middle of a verbal dispute. The man came forward with his long night robe and a small flashlight in his left hand.

"I am sorry but we were just passing by?"

"Really, then please don't shout." The man with the light said in a pissed manner. "Who are you guys?"

"Well, we're police, so just go back inside. We'll leave in a bit." Blake replied. "And can you please lower the light as it's burning my eyes."

The man lowered the flash and was now more visible to the two. He had a round face, short hair, and a slightly darker tone. He was carrying a small pistol in his secret pocket in case things were supposed to be deceitful.

"Don't worry sir, we are here for a reason?"

"And that is?" The man was getting worried about the two anonymous people.

Dave intervened. "We're looking for Mr Henry."

"What for?"

"We're representing the police and want to talk with Henry regarding a case."

"Don't you think you're a little early." The man said sarcastically.

The two smiled back. "Well, when we started our journey it was still daylight."

"Alright." The man was more comfortable. "So where are you from?"

"We came from Pinewood."

"Really?" He replied astonishingly. 'That's pretty far from here."

"Indeed it is," Blake replied, putting his phone in his pocket. "I think it's reasonable information from our end."

"Well, you're talking to Henry."

Dave was not so surprised upon hearing the man as if he knew about him already. "I had some notion."

"Me too." Blake also agreed.

"So, are you here to arrest me?" Henry asked in a casual tone. "Because I know a lot about law and warrants."

"No sir, we just want to know about Rick."

The man looked confused and didn't speak for a few seconds. "You mean Richard?

"Yes! I guess he was called Rick in Pinewood."

"What's wrong? Is he alright?"

Blake looked at Dave and went right back to Henry. "Well, he's missing."

"Oh God, what happened?"

Blake took a deep breath. "A lot." He paused for a bit. "Sir, can we talk about this inside because it's getting pretty cold out here?"

"Sure. Follow my lead."

The three entered the small house and sat on the sofas in the living room. Henry had a labrador who seemed pretty old and slow. He didn't even bother to look at the strangers. The two sat, and Henry brought them some hot tea.

"Thank you." Dave took his cup and kept it on the wooden table.

"You have a lovely dog," Blake said as he tried to pet the old pal.

"Well he's a good boy." Henry immediately came back to the matter. "So, please tell me what happened?"

"First of all, I would like to know—are you related to Richard?"

"No, he was my associate in an electrical project in the town a few years back. I have known him since then. He's a good, hard working guy."

"Alright." Blake took a deep breath. "Well, he's missing."

Henry was baffled and couldn't believe what he was hearing. "I mean, how? When? What happened?"

"Well, your friend found himself in the middle of a case we're investigating. He might be a leading suspect or a victim, and now he's gone."

"Actually, he found a dead person in Pinewood and alerted the authorities, but then we went to talk with him. However, he was not present and it turns out he gave a lot of wrong information to his landlord." Dave added to make things more clear.

"Oh, God, that's bad."

"So, do you know where he is?" Blake came straight to the point.

"Unfortunately, it's been some time since we both talked." Henry paused. "He was busy on the farm meanwhile I have my own stuff to do, so you know, it's been a while."

"Alright." Blake continued. "But what about his family? I mean, do you know if he got one?"

"I don't know much about his background. He came to this town from the city. And whenever we tried to talk about families—he always changed the subject."

Blake laughed and looked at Dave. "You believe this guy?"

Dave had no idea what to say or interpret. "I don't know detective."

"So, you're saying that you don't know anything of matter about him."

"Sir, I am telling you everything I know." Henry said in his defence. Blake was getting frustrated. However, he tried to control his nerves. He pulled a cigarette and left the house.

"I think that's enough for today." Dave said before leaving as well. "Detective? What's wrong?"

Blake inhaled the smoke from his cigarette and sighed. "He's lying." He pointed towards the house. "The man knows something, but he's playing a little naive sucker." Blake looked at Dave. "I am going to use a different method of interrogation." He took a last puff, opened his jacket, and rolled his sleeves. Dave hurriedly held him back to his car.

"Detective, this is not the right way to do things."

"I don't care anymore," Blake said angrily while Henry looked from the gap between the curtains.

"I mean look at him, peeping through the holes." Blake pointed towards the man.

"Don't worry, we'll get him; you need some sleep." Dave tried to talk down the Detective. "Let's get out of here."

They both sat in the car and drove away. Dave called a nearby hotel to stay the night and plan further about the situation.

Both were silent. Dave was busy on his phone while Blake was smoking like a maniac. He snapped, and now he was conscious of his act. They might have blundered their chance to move forward in the case through Henry. He will be more alert about the two of them if he knows something.

"I am sorry, man, for being a jerk back there. I don't know what happened?"

"No worries captain, we'll get him sooner or later." Dave consoled the demoralised Detective. "But what makes you sure that he's our guy?"

"Man, I have been doing this for more than 10 years. I have worked with the best and solved many cases. I just know. He was blatantly lying to our faces and there's nothing we can do about it."

"So, what's the play going ahead?"

"I don't know Dave, maybe keep tabs on him I guess."

"But he's alerted no?"

"Hmmm, we'll see about that." Blake sighed and fell back on the bed. "I think he knows Rick's location."

"Really?" Dave asked like an associate and a rational person.

"I bet on my life."

"Well, I won't go that far but it's a possibility."

"Yes, it's certain. Look, I'll have to be here for some time. So, if you want to go back you can go tomorrow."

"What do you mean?" Dave was confused.

"I have to keep 24x7 tabs on Henry. I need to follow him and see what comes next."

"But Detective, this will probably take a long time." He paused. "Days, I guess, but who knows."

"So what should I do in the meantime?"

"Hmmm, I guess work with your friend Simon and look for Ella." He stood up. "Look, I don't know how long it will take for me to solve this case and I don't want to keep you occupied for no reason. If you can work on your case—feel free to do so."

"I understand but what if you need assistance here?"

"Don't worry I'll keep you posted and will call you when the time is right."

Dave understood Blake's reasoning, as there was no point in wasting time on a single person when there were other angles to explore. However, he wanted to help Blake, who was clearly on to something in the current investigation.

"Detective, I will stick with you." He continued to explain. "Look, I don't know anything about the investigation, as the last time I tried to do anything, I was behind bars. So, I should stick with you and clear up this case before it becomes a mess."

Blake was glad to hear that. "Thanks man, I appreciate it." He nodded at Dave. "Let's get started."

The following day, the two decided to visit Henry's place. He was still inside and probably getting ready for work. The man worked with a local contractor and was in charge of some housing projects in Ivory Town. They followed him the entire time and noted his schedule.

He had no family and was seen hanging out with many of his co-workers after his shift. He came home at around 10 at night after hanging in one of the bars. Besides a typical day at work, he was rarely seen doing anything suspicious. However, Blake contacted one of his friends to pull Henry's mobile records, only to find that he received some random calls every day during the afternoon. The duration of those calls was around 2-3 minutes max, and it had been like this for a couple of weeks. Thus, the two of them grow more suspicious of Henry but can't afford to lose their lead by being careless.

Dave was still in touch with Simon, who was back in Pinewood looking over Ella's case. However, there was no progress from his side, which Dave had expected from the first day.

The two investigators waited in their car just outside Henry's work site. It was a big building in its final stages. The suspect was in charge of electrical wiring throughout the area.

"Do you think we're wasting our time on Henry?" Dave asked impatiently.

"Yes and no, I guess."

"What the hell does that mean?"

"Dave, he's smart and patient and what we need is to be more patient than him." He sighed. "He'll make a mistake, I am certain of that. It's the matter of when?"

Dave was uncomfortable in his hometown. He was scared to run across his family members or even a familiar face. Meanwhile, the cost of living in a hotel was terminating his credit card limit. They need to make some progress in the case, or it will be impossible for Dave to continue the investigation. Days passed, and there was nothing new on the case apart from the same investigative routine.

"Detective, it's been a week but we don't have anything on Henry apart from those strange calls."

"I know but we can't give up now. We're so close to him."

"But what if he knows that we're following him? That's horrible for us. Maybe he's tricking us everyday."

"It can be, but we are very cautious. I don't think he knows about us." Blake tried his best to come up with valid answers. He also knew that they both were having money problems and stretching the tabs on Henry really affected their budget and timeline. They were resourceful for only a couple of more days.

"I don't know for how long I can do this." Dave sounded desperate. He was sick and tired from doing nothing the whole day. His patience and composure had reached all its limits.

The day passed, and there was still no progress. The next day, the two followed Henry on his schedule. However, he took a different turn this time. He drove his grey SUV to a remote area. He was already pretty far from his usual workplace.

Blake and Dave drove behind but kept a reasonable distance to keep their cover. After following him for over thirty minutes—they arrived at a small gas station. Henry refuelled his car and bought some items from the store.

Before moving further, he called someone from his cell phone. It was a small chat that lasted for probably one or two minutes. Their suspicion grew even more as they swiftly followed the man through the country's rough roads. After briefly following the guy for over an hour, he stopped at a roadside motel. He parked his car, took out the groceries and entered the building. After waiting for over 30 minutes outside the motel, Henry came outside and hurriedly drove away. However, Blake decided not to follow him. They waited for Henry to get out of sight and then went inside. They were welcomed by a man at the entrance who was in charge of the building. He wore shabby clothes and was a chubby man with a big beard and a grey cap.

"Can I help you?" He said in a welcoming tone.

"Yes, we're from the police department and are working on a case," Blake replied as he showed his expired police batch. Dave looked around the place and could sense a moisturising smell. The man was intimidated by their presence.

"I am sorry sir but we are a legitimate site."

"I know, and I am not here for your business. I am looking for a man." Blake showed him pictures of Rick. The man saw the photo and instantly recognised him.

"Sir, he's here."

Blake took back the photograph. "You know him."

"Yes, he booked a room here for some time."

"And what about the guy who you just talked to?."

"You mean Henry."

"Yes, where did he go?"

"He left after a few minutes."

The man nodded positively with a bit of guilty expression. He hesitated to give the officers such valuable information, but he had no choice.

"How'd you know these people?"

"I don't know them personally but since they often come here I know about them."

"Please tell us the truth," Blake said politely. These guys are not the people you want to associate with and trust me, I won't do anything to you."

"Sir, this is all I know."

The Detective paused for a bit. "Alright, take us to his room."

"Sure. Come this way." He pointed in the inner direction and took his card with him. The two followed the man until he stopped in front of a wooden door. He knocked a couple of times, but there was no response. So, the Detective asked him to open the door without any hesitation. He took out the key and unlocked the door.

They all entered the place, and it was a mess. There was a bed and a couple of chairs—the television was one, and the room smelled of booze and smoke. Rick was in the bathroom, so he couldn't hear them.

The Detective asked the man to wait outside the room. As Rick stepped outside the small bathroom, he was surprised to see them—he couldn't even react to the situation as he held a toothbrush in his right hand.

"No more hiding Rick," Blake said with a broad smile. "It's time to go back home."

The man devastatingly sat on the bed and put his hands on his head; he was caught, and he could do nothing about it.

XIII

Statements

After finding Rick, Blake charged Henry with not negotiating with the authorities, but he was not their problem. They brought Rick back to Pinewood, where the police thoroughly investigated him.

Blake led the investigation and was also in charge of the interrogation. Dave was left out of the scenario, considering he was not a police officer. Rick didn't say much after his arrest. However, it was only a matter of time before he faced Blake's wrath.

Blake came into the station to chat with Rick. He went into a small interrogation room where Rick was waiting for him. The detective sat across the silent man with a malicious look.

"So nice to you finally." Blake smiled. "It was really hard to get hold of you."

"Is this a joke?" Rick finally broke his silence. "Why have you brought me in? I have done nothing wrong."

"Oh, really! Then why did you disappear? Hmm, do you have any explanation?"

"I had no choice."

"Tell me more about it." Blake leaned a bit forward. "Listen, I still don't know what you've done but it's better for you to say what you know and then we'll see what I can do about it—please no more lies."

"Sir, I am telling you I am just an eye witness."

"Then tell me what happened?"

Rick was getting a bit scared, but he took a breath and continued.

"So, I was coming back from the town's market to my place. It was a long day, and I needed some rest. As I was on my way, I saw a man lying on his back on the side of the road. At first, I thought of leaving since he might be an alcoholic, but then I noticed blood on the back of his head. Then I called the police, and yes, that's what happened."

"Did you see anyone else?"

There was silence, which frustrated Blake and resulted in him stomping the table. "Enough of this nonsense. You think you're smart—sooner or later, you'll be behind bars."

"But I did not do anything." Rick cried, and for a second, Blake thought he might be telling the truth.

"Then why did you run?"

"Because I was told to!"

Blake realised and said. "Wait, are you being threatened?"

Rick looked at him and then lowered his face. He then lifted his sleeve and showed some bruises on his right arm and his back.

"What happened?" Blake asked calmly as he felt terrible for the guy. "Listen, you don't have to worry. You'll be safe. Trust me, I can guarantee that."

"Oh god, they might kill me." Rick continued. "I was walking to the town. It was one day after the murder. Then, all of a sudden, I was attacked from behind. They were multiple people, I guess. I didn't see them as I was covering my face. And one of them told me to leave the city or meet the same fate." Rick was crying. "I didn't want to die, but I was alone in the town. So, I called Henry and asked him to arrange for me in Ivory Town. And that's that."

Blake is confused and partial about Rick's narrative but decides to believe him. However, he is still in their custody for further investigation.

"Alright, but why would they want to hurt you? Did you see or know about anything that is suspicious?"

"I don't know, but before I saw the dead man on the road. I passed a girl, probably 25. She looked at me but instantly took out her phone. She was in a hurry, and her clothes were pretty shabby."

"What was she wearing exactly?"

"I can't recall, but it seemed as if I had seen her before."

"Can you recognise her face?" Blake pulled out a photo from his jacket and showed it to Rick. "Did you see her?"

Rick took a long look at the photo and confirmed it was her.

"Are you a hundred percent sure?" Blake wanted to take no chances.

"I think it's her."

"Thanks, I'll talk to you later and you're free to go."

"But detective, what about my safety?"

Blake stood and looked at him. "Call Henry and sort it through but stay in touch with me. I'll arrange something if I can. And if anything comes up, I am the one you'll call. Understand?"

"Alright." Rick was not pleased with the detective, but at least he was free and needed protection and hiding.

Blake called Dave and asked him to meet at his place. Dave was in his apartment, and there was not much going on then. He immediately got ready to meet the detective. He reached before him and waited on the outside street. The detective came, parked his car and asked Dave to follow him upstairs.

"So, what is it? Did you find anything?" Dave was curious to know.

"Yes, there's good and bad news for you?" Blake put his coat on the sofa and continued. "Ella is alive, but she might be in danger."

Dave couldn't believe what he heard. It was a blow to his head, and he couldn't fathom the statement.

"Wait a sec." He stuttered to put on a sentence. "I don't understand."

"Here, take a seat," Blake asked Dave, and he explained the entire situation to him. It was also shocking for the detective, but he was familiar with such conditions.

"But detective, the man could be lying!" Dave spoke after digesting the entire news.

"You're right, but I don't see that because Rick seemed frightened and had no advantage to fool us. I mean, he's in danger, and at the moment, we are the only ones who can help him."

"So, what do we do now? If Ella is still alive, then the two cases are related, and finding Ella is the only way to solve this mess. She has to know something about this case."

"Yes," Blake said and lit a cigarette. "I think we need to start from the other side of the case."

He brought in a board and started laying out all the evidence, names, and locations they had on the murder case. It was all coming together; however, most of this case didn't make sense. Dave had no idea what was happening in the town. It was a relieving and frightening experience for Dave since he was not the only one who saw Ella.

Detective Blake carefully evaluated and investigated what he had on a case. After hours, he was ready with a strategy to approach the situation.

"Dave, what are you up to?" The detective asked Dave, who was busy on the phone with Simon. Apparently, he told everything that he knew at the time. This gossip made Blake mad as he didn't trust anyone except Dave.

"I am sorry, I was just talking to Simon." He hung up his cell phone. "So, what's the plan?"

"What's the plan?" The detective cried in frustration. "Why the hell are you broadcasting our entire case?"

"But detective, he's my friend."

"I don't care if it's your friend or spouse. Don't talk to anybody about the case except for me. Am I clear?"

Dave realised his mistake and understood the gravity of the situation. Even though he trusted Simon, he couldn't take any chances. "I am sorry."

There was silence for a minute or two before Blake stood up and went to his room. He came back with a long coat.

"Come on, we're leaving." The detective asked Dave to follow his lead.

"Where to?"

"Silver Lake." He paused for a bit. "I have some questions for Mr and Mrs Cooper."

"Alright but is it safe for me to go with you?" Dave was recalling his prior experience.

"Sure, you'll be fine." He took his wallet from the table. "Only that doctor has a problem with you but we'll make sure to avoid him."

"Ok." Dave nodded. "Let's go."

The two left for Silver Lake without wasting much time. It was the second time Blake would see the Cooper family. He knew about them and Ella's disappearance case but never worked on it. But now Ella is a suspect based on the statement of a critical victim. And even if she's innocent, her appearance around a dead person is still questionable, considering she was missing for over a year.

They reached the Cooper family. Mrs Cooper opened the door; he was surprised to see the detective but frowned upon Dave. She wasn't expecting the two after Dave's altercation the previous week.

"Detective, " she looked back inside. Mr. Cooper was holding the cell phone in his hand. He stood up from his seat at the sight of the two individuals.

"Why are you here?" He asked from the inside with an irritating tone.

"We are here because we have some news and a few questions for you."

The couple looked at one another and ultimately decided to welcome their uninvited guests. They sat in front of Mr Cooper.

"Dave, you hired a detective to find Ella." Mr Cooper was disappointed, as if he was sick of the entire drama.

"Well, we were working on Ella's case but something else came up."

"What?" He cried in frustration.

Blake pitched to calm the situation. "Listen Mr and Mrs Cooper. You guys are nice people since you helped me in a rough situation—considering you guys were suffering as well. And trust me when Dave came to me and said that he saw Ella on a couple of different occasions, I couldn't believe him as well. But something unexpected happened in the investigation of my other case."

"What is it?" The Coopers asked in synchronisation.

"Well, one of the key witnesses has seen Ella near the murder scene."

The Coopers were shocked upon hearing the news. They couldn't have imagined such news at the time. "You're mistaken." Mr Cooper said in a low voice. "It's not possible."

"Why would you say that?" Dave broke his silence. "Our source has confirmed her presence at the scene. Now, it's your turn to give us some answers."

"Oh God, what do you want from us?"

"The truth." Detective Blake said as he opened his diary.

The two were speechless. However, the investigators gave them some time to think about the situation.

"Ella was supposed to be dead because of her heart condition. The doctors gave her around 6-8 months." Mr Cooper continued. "Over the course of time, we were privately looking for some of the best doctors in the region. And after dozens of appointments, we came to the conclusion that it was her fate to die of the disorder."

"We were so lost at the time." Mrs Cooper started. "I mean it was hard for us to think about the future. However, one of the major surgeons in the city suggested a heart transplant."

"But the probability and success rate of such a critical procedure was less than one percent." Mr Cooper stood up and went to a nearby drawer. He took out the file and showed it to Blake. It had different opinions or suggestions from the doctors.

"After that, there was the issue of heart donors." He sat back in his seat. "You know, there are not a lot of donors in the country plus the complexity of the operation was too much for us to take such a risk." He had tears in his eyes. "So, yes, I don't think that your man saw Ella because she'd be dead by now."

'But what if she got a transplant?' Dave asked as he peered at the files Blake was holding in his hand.

"How so? I mean she can't do that on her own. She didn't have the resources."

"Then why did she run off?" Dave said in a blameful manner. "You don't think she can arrange something on her own?"

"I hope she did, but I don't know what to say," Mr Cooper said as he looked at his wife. They were both disappointed and had no conclusive ideas about the situation.

"Well, the evidence suggests that Ella is still alive and I just want you two to alert us in case she tries to make any contact." The detective stood up. "I know it's hard and harsh for you but it's best if you trust us on this one."

Both of them nodded, and Blake seemed assured. Dave followed his associate but had an aggressive expression on his face. He was still suspicious of the family, and that particular cloud of judgment was not easy to ignore.

"That's all," Dave asked the detective, who was lighting a cigarette.

He looked back. "What do you mean?"

"They were clearly hiding something. We should have been more persuasive."

"Maybe but not this time. Let them sink in the news." Blake calmly explained to Dave.

"So what now?"

"Nothing, just go back to Pinewood." Blake continued as he took a puff. "Let's look into the dead guy and your girl. Maybe there is some connection between the two."

"You think so?"

"Yes, I mean she was present at the site of murder. And by that rationale it's not wrong to assume that she might be related to her."

Dave was trying his best to keep Ella away from the murder case. Still, all the fundamental investigations pointed to her link with Philip's murder. They both went back to Pinewood. It was a tiring day for them. Nothing happened in between their travels. Simon was waiting for his friend; however, Dave was careful when sharing the information regarding the case.

The detective dropped Dave at his place and asked him to meet in the morning. Upon reaching his apartment, Simon welcomed Blake.

"How's it going?" He greeted his friend.

"Good, just a bit tired from travelling." Dave noticed that Simon was ready with a suitcase. "You're going somewhere."

"Yes, I am going back to the city. My mother is sick, and I need to be with her."

"Really, is she ok? What happened?"

"Yes, it's just a fever, but I want to take precautions, so it's better if I am with her—taking care of the household stuff."

"I understand—so when are you leaving?" Dave relaxed on a couch.

Simon looked at his clock. "In about two hours. It's a night train so I'll be home by tomorrow morning."

"That's great." Dave said with a low voice.

"Hey, don't worry, I'll be back."

"Nah, nah, it's ok. I am just a bit tired, nothing else. You have a safe trip."

"Thanks man, and, there is some pizza left in the kitchen in case you're hungry."

Dave was stuck between two moods—one desired pizza while the other wanted to sleep. He chose to go to his room and rest. He hugged Simon, knowing he'd be gone when he woke again.

It was early morning, and Dave had slept the whole night. As soon as he woke up, he looked at his phone for updates. There were a bunch of useless emails, but nothing substantial. He got fresh and ate the leftovers for breakfast.

By then, he received a text from the detective, who asked him to reach Philip's store by 10 o'clock. There was still time, so he returned to the case. At that point, there were no particular advancements in the case apart from its relation to Ella. Dave decided to meet Rick to ensure the current situation's validity. He wanted to hear from the man himself, as he was the only other person who saw Ella.

Rick was hiding for safety; only the detective knew about his location. He told Dave and asked him to keep it a secret. The detective even arranged a cell phone number for Rick so that he couldn't be traced easily.

At first, Dave thought of calling the man, but it wasn't an excellent way to investigate him. So, he went to his place or the secret hiding place. He called him to alert him of his arrival. It was a one-story abandoned apartment in the south end of the town. No one was around the place, as it was a remote location.

Dave entered the place and looked for Rick, who was busy watching some news on the television. Upon seeing Dave, Richard muted the set and stood up. He was a bit scared and irritated by Dave's presence, but his plan was working since it was the first time they had met. Rick extended his hand to greet the young gun.

"You're with the Detective."

"Rick, how are you?"

"I am fine, Mr-." He looked confused.

"You can call me Dave. Would you mind?" Dave sat on a wooden stool. "So, how are you holding up?"

"To be honest, I don't like this. I mean I am being threatened by some unknown entities and even the police are not doing a decent job. Look at this place, it's more frightening than the outside."

"I can understand but it's for your safety." Dave continued. "Trust me, we will find the people behind all this mess and soon you'll be safe."

"Don't make promises Dave because none of this makes any sense." Rick sighed and looked disappointed. "So, why are you here? Don't you have a case to work on?"

"I am here because I needed to talk to you about the girl that you saw." Blake took out a picture from his wallet. "I know you've probably saw her before but are you 100 percent sure that its her?"

He looked at the photograph and immediately nodded positively.

"Alright, but how can you remember her so clearly?" Dave asked as he put the wallet back in his pocket.

"What kind of question is that?" Rick replied in frustration.

"You do understand what I am trying to ask you. So don't be silly and answer me, why are you twisting the words?"

Rick couldn't believe the guy. "Look man, I don't know who you are and your role in this case but I am not talking to you anymore." He sat while ignoring the guy. This pissed Dave, and he angrily punched the TV screen. It broke down, and Rick was speechless. After Dave left the house, a black car drove to the back street with tinted windows. He was about to call Blake to wait for him, but then he heard a gunshot inside the house. He stopped and turned around, but then someone sneaked from the back and landed a massive blow to the side of his head. He was unconscious, and the last thing he remembered was seeing a shadow in front of him.

XIV
Recovery

Dave woke up in the hospital. The detective sat before him. Elliot was also there. He was the one looking after the arrangements, which was very unexpected. His head was covered with a crepe bandage, and it still hurt him. However, with the remaining strength and Elliot's help, he sat up and leaned on back support.

"I am sorry Detective." Dave said slowly as he recalled the situation. "I shouldn't have been there."

"It's alright. We're glad you're safe." He looked at Elliot, who stood at the side of the bed.

"And what about Rick?" He panicked. "My God, I heard a gunshot and it was all black."

The detective looked disappointed. Elliot was silent as well. Dave realised he messed up.

"What happened to him?" The detective tried to paddle the conversation. "Dave, you should rest. We'll talk about the case when you're fully recovered."

"Oh, come on, I am fine. Just tell me what happened?"

"Alright." The detective asked Elliot to give them some time. The case was confidential, and he didn't want anyone involved for security reasons.

"Look Dave, it's been over 12 hours that you've been admitted here. You woke up a couple of times before but the Doctor asked us to leave you alone. That day, you were found on the outside of Rick's hiding place while he was dead inside. Apparently, someone shot him in the head."

"Yes, I heard the gunshot but as soon as I moved inside, I was hit badly." Dave was silent for a second. "Damnit, it's my fault."

"No, it's not."

"It is. You asked me to come to your place that day, but I was a little skeptical of Rick's statement against Ella, so I decided to interrogate him myself." He was disappointed. "Maybe someone followed me. I don't know." Tears came in his eyes. "Probably an innocent man died because of me."

"Hey, look at me." The detective said in a severe tone. "In this line of work, you can't think like this. It doesn't help. And as far as I am concerned, we have a lot of work to do."

Dave thought for a bit and then agreed with his partner. "Let's go then." He tried to stand and recollect himself but was too tired.

"You need rest for now. Let the drugs wear off and then we'll see. Alright?" Blake asked as he helped Dave to lie on his back. "I'll see you later."

Dave tried his best to hear more from Blake. "Can you share anything about the case? I mean Rick. Is there anything suspicious."

Blake stood at the door. "We'll talk about that." He left, and Dave was disappointed. As Blake left, Elliot came inside. He was still slightly upset about his friendship with Dave but wanted to do right by him.

"Hey, how are you doing?" Elliot took a seat by Dave.

"I am good, thanks for asking." He looked around. "And that's for being here. It means a lot."

Elliot nodded as he understood his friend. "Look, man, I know things are not right between us, but I want to say that you should go back. Coming from me, I don't want you to lose your life. I tried my best to keep your situation away from your family and even Simon, but this is it. This is your last chance to leave this all behind and start again."

"I am sorry for some mistakes but you know I can't do that. I am too deep in this now and going back is not an option."

"I knew you would say that, but it was my duty to tell you as a long lost friend." Elliot stood up and left the room. Dave thought for a bit about his situation, but the medications made him fall asleep once again. He woke up the next day and was ready to leave. Doctors gave him some prescriptions, and all his bills were paid by Elliot, who had already gone as soon as he saw that Dave was good to go. Detective Blake came to pick up his partner. His car stood right outside the hospital. After collecting his items and doing a bunch of formalities, Dave was set to get back on the investigation. However, he still thought about what Elliot had said the night before. As soon as he entered the car, Blake realised that something was off about Dave.

"You good?" He asked as he drove the man back to his place.

"I am good, just, a bit sedated."

"Don't worry, it will wear off."

"Where are we going?"

"First, we're going to your place. You should sort your stuff and freshen up. In the meantime, I have to meet someone from the forensics department."

"Is it about Rick?"

"Yes, an old associate of mine will give me some reports regarding his wounds. So, I'll look into it and get back to you."

"Sound goods to me." Dave sighed and stared through the window.

Blake tried his best to lift Dave's spirit.

"Look, Dave." He continued. "You don't have to do this. I mean, your life is in danger."

"But so yours?" He replied immediately.

"Its different for me."

"How so?"

"Well, for starters I don't have people around. All my career I've worked professionally without any hindrance from personal life. And also, it's my job. None of this implies for you."

"I get it but now I really want to do this."

"What if something happened to you? I don't want to be the one who faces the aftermath."

"You don't have to do that."

"Look, I just want to say that I am dropping you at your place. Think about the situation and make up your mind. I won't ask again. Your friend at the hospital wants the same for you."

Blake dropped Dave at his place and left to meet someone from the forensic team. Dave was tired, nauseous and even in pain. He entered his place and lay on the couch—his phone was dead, and he put it on a charger. Immediately, there were some messages and call notifications. He looked at those, and most were from Simon; maybe he got to know his situation through Elliot.

Nonetheless, he decided to silence his device and let it be. The past few hours have been difficult for him, making him question his path. In a few days, he's been in a police station once and twice in the hospital. Was this all a warning to retreat or a sign that he was heading towards the truth?

Everyone around him was asking to leave it all behind, but Dave didn't want to give up. In deep thought, he suddenly fell asleep at his place. Maybe it was a dream or a memory, but he suddenly remembered something—the car with tinted windows. All his sleep vanished within a few seconds, and he called Blake. Unfortunately, the detective didn't pick up his phone and had no idea where he was going. So, there was no other option for him but to wait. However, he was impatient and wanted to sort this out. Therefore, he decided to walk the streets searching for a black-tinted car.

Pinewood was a small town, but all this changed if you walked. Even though Dave knew about the town, it was still difficult for him to navigate the entire place. He also was waiting for the detective to call him back. He could've used his little car to make his search more effortless. After walking for several hours around the town, Dave was lost and tired. He sat on a public bench, looking at the strangers passing him. It was almost evening, and there was still no sign of the detective. The day's disappointment took over Dave, who was bewildered by the people around him. After sitting for a few minutes, he decided to head back, but a man in a long coat stood before him. It was Jade, who was looking at Dave with curiosity as if he was trying to remember him.

"You are with the detective on my brother's case. Or am I mistaken?" He asked as he took a seat beside Dave.

"You're right. I am his associate."

"What was it again? I am sorry I didn't remember your name."

"No problem. It's Dave." They both shook hands.

"So, what are you doing here?" Jade asked as he leaned back on the bench.

"Nothing, the detective has gone to meet a forensic expert. Meanwhile, I am just doing my job."

"I see, so, is there any update on Philip's case?"

"I am sorry but I can't disclose anything right now." Dave dismissed the question.

"I understand but today I read about Rick in the local newspaper. It's frightening to be honest. I mean, people are getting murdered left and right." Jade said in a concerned voice.

"That's a tragedy. I was there." Dave paused for a bit. He couldn't speak about Rick. "I should probably head back but if something comes up I'll let you know." Dave hurriedly stood up and headed back. Jade couldn't believe his eyes and just sat there.

As Dave started to head back to his place, he finally got a call from the detective, who asked him to meet at a local bar. He was relieved to hear from Blake as his tension grew exponentially throughout the day. He reached the place in half an hour—called the "Bright Bar"- which was ironic considering the people leaving were drunk. He saw Blake with a beer on one of the seats.

The detective welcomed his partner and ordered some drinks for him as well.

"How are you?" Dave sat beside him. "I am sorry I couldn't reach you during the day."

"It's ok. I just wanted to tell you something."

"Go ahead."

Dave told Blake about the car he saw at Rick's place. Blake was not surprised to hear this. However, he felt terrible that Dave had to look for the vehicle all day while walking on the street.

"Don't worry, I'll inform the police about the vehicle."

Dave was finally relieved, plus his drink came as well." So, what did the expert say about Rick?"

"Well, the forensic report clearly suggested that he was shot from behind. So, I guess the shooter was right behind him. There were other technical assumptions, but that was it. Nothing worth your concern."

Blake sighed and closed his eyes momentarily.

"Another dead end, I guess," Dave remarked disappointedly.

Blake immediately opened his eyes. "No, we're on the right track; that's why Rick died. He came to us and paid the price. That's all."

"But don't you think we got him killed."

"Truth comes at a price." Blake dismissed Dave's excuse. "Plus, you shouldn't have been there."

Dave was silent, and Blake regretted his choice of words. "Look man, the world is full of actions and sometimes things don't go our way but it doesn't mean we stop acting the way we're supposed to. You thought about something which seemed right. No shame in that. Also, you shouldn't be here in the first place. It's not your job. So, don't blame yourself all over again."

Dave nodded as if he understood some bit of the pep talk. "But you think someone is spying on us?"

"Did anyone know that you are going to Rick's?" Blake asked and continued. "What about your friend?"

"Simon, nah, he left the place the night before." Dave immediately dismissed the notion.

"Why?"

"His mother is not well."

"Oh, I see." He paused for a bit. "But did you see him leaving for home? Or on a train? How can you be so sure?"

"Seriously Detective?" Dave couldn't believe his ears. "You're trying to frame my friend. After all he's been through for me."

"I am not framing. I am just asking the questions which you're very oblivious to ask."

"Oh come on." Dave was pissed. "I should head back. I'll meet you in the morning."

"Later." The detective didn't press on the issue.

Dave left the bar without drinking. However, thinking about Simon made him realise he should call him back. He tried reaching his friend, but unfortunately, he didn't pick up his phone. It made Dave suspicious of Simon since he always picked up his phone. He was walking to his apartment, and it began to drizzle a bit, and the whole town became dull and grey. Dave had to stop beneath a balcony of a two-storey store—he didn't want to get wet and challenge his immunity. Standing at the spot, he saw many people following his steps and taking shelter under the buildings. It was all peaceful, as if time stood still for the moment. Dave, for the first time in a long time, felt peace and tranquillity—thanks to the drops of nature. He had no sense of time, and everything became foggy. A rain shelter was at a distance; under it, he saw a familiar face. A girl in a long coat and black jeans sat on the bench. No one else was around her, and for a time, Dave thought she was simulated. Nonetheless, he left his place and moved towards her. As he reached her place, Ella was already waiting for him.

"Take a seat." She asked Dave to rest beside her.

"Is this true?" Dave couldn't believe her eyes. The reality of the situation was paramount.

"Does it matter?" She asked with a monotonous voice.

"I don't know." He sat down. "You are alive?"

"You should leave this place now."

"Why'd you say that?" He sounded exasperated.

"Your life is in danger."

"What do you mean?"

And just like that, a considerable thunderbolt stumbled into the vast sky. Dave shook his head in amazement, and the girl was long gone. He stood on the side of the road, soaking wet from head to toe. The rain had stopped, and the town was back to normal.

Dave was still amused about the incident and had no explanation. Blake tried to reach him on his cellphone, but he didn't answer. Everything was a mess, and Dave just wanted to escape this situation. He reached his place and rested for a bit. He was asleep for over an hour; however, his sleep was affected by the ringing phone. Simon was calling him back. He picked up his friend's phone and talked for a bit. Dave took Simon's update. His mother was sick, so he might not return to Pinewood for another week. This made Dave a bit disappointed, but his suspicion downfolded.

Simon was not on to something; maybe Blake was right to doubt everyone. Perhaps it's the way to investigate. Such thoughts ramble across Dave's mind, but he has no notion of his next act.

A part of him wanted to leave the town once and for all, but the other side craved truth and meaning. His past was full of mystery, which his present didn't want to get rid of.

Ultimately, he called Blake and asked him to pick him up from his apartment. The detective was in the neighbourhood and came to see his associate.

"You good?" Blake asked the tiring-looking Dave.

"I am great, let's get back to work."

"Sure."

"Did you reach your friend?"

Dave looked at the detective with a bitter expression. "How'd you know that?"

"Because I have been doing this stuff for over ten years. But forget it." He paused. "So, what did he say?"

"Well, he's still in the city, taking care of his mother and might return after a week or so."

"Alright." The detective thought for a bit. "But why is he helping you?"

"Really." Dave was annoyed. "He's my friend. Just helping me through some tough times."

"I get it but it's too good to be true."

"Well, Detective, that's not my problem. Maybe you never had a good friend in your life. Maybe it's your voracious nature."

The detective was speechless, and Dave realised he was harsh with his companion. They didn't talk more about the subject. Blake drove to a nearby cafe, where someone was waiting for him. It was Henry, who was still mourning his dead friend. Blake took care of Henry's charges in return for facilitating the investigation. They both sat in front of him. The man was upset and clearly lost.

"Henry." Dave greeted the man. "How are you holding up?"

"I am fine sir."

"Would you like something to drink?" Blake asked generously. Dave looked at the silent man in front of him.

"No thanks. I am good." Words took a toll coming out of his mouth.

"Dave, you need something."

"Coffee will be good."

Blake pointed to the reception. "Alright, then order one for me as well." Dave had no idea that Blake was this broke. Nevertheless, he ordered two lattes for him and the detective. At that point, the detective was already having a conversation with Henry. He immediately rushed to the table to avoid missing essential details. As he sat, he realised they both were just conversing over the dead man.

"I don't know detective. Do I thank you for freeing me or blame you for what happened to Rick?"

"Henry, look, I know he was your friend and maybe I was wrong to put you in custody. But I had no choice." He paused for a bit. "Forget it, I am deeply sorry for what happened? But you have to realise that Rick was probably involved in some shady business."

"To hell with your apologies." Henry burst into anger, making the whole crowd look at him. Blake smiled at the crowd to make things less awkward for them.

"I know that you're sad and angry for your friend's loss but you have to help us."

"Oh yeah." He glared at the detective. "What do you want to know from me?"

"Everything that you know about Rick."

"Seriously." He paused. "I told you everything already. And you said that he'd be safe. Now, I should ask you what happened to your promise."

Blake was speechless as he couldn't reason with the truth. "It was my fault. I should have cared for your friend, but let me ask you one thing. Was he safe at that hotel? Was he feeling comfortable with his stay? No—he was still in danger, and I get it; it's not an excuse for what happened but to my understanding he had a bounty on his shoulder. It was only a matter of when. So, just help us to get your late friend justice."

Henry didn't say a word for a bit. Things were getting awkward between them. Dave was trying his best to focus on his coffee. Meanwhile, Blake was staring at the man in front of him. It was a sort of motivating technique, or so Dave believed.

Finally, Henry started to lay out some additional details. "Rick saw the dead man and called the police force. However, he also saw a girl coming from the same direction. But that's not all for the incident."

Dave and Blake both were listening attentively to the man. "He not only saw the girl but there was also a man in the incident."

"Is he the murderer?"

"He was not sure but he was definitely sure that the same man threatened him after he laid a beating on him to keep him off the case."

"Did you know how he looked?" Blake asked curiously.

"No detective. I asked Rick a couple of times but he said that he'll be putting my life at risk if he speaks of him."

"But still, there has to be something about the man." He was a bit dissatisfied.

"I am sorry but whatever it was, it passed away with Rick."

Henry laid his head in his hands and sat remorsefully. He wished to know more about the deceased, but maybe Rick was trying to protect him. Upon this revelation, the two investigators had two suspects. One was Ella, and the other was the unknown man who probably worked alongside her on whatever they were up to.

The detective lets the man be alone and asks Dave to leave. They were both outside the shop, and Blake lit a cigarette. Without the man's identity or any details, it was nearly impossible to track him. However, plenty of details still needed attention from the two. Dave kept wondering about Ella's role in all this. It was not clear to him that she could possibly not only be alive but involved in two murders. Something about all this does not make sense to him. He waited for the detective to decide their next move. At present, he was busy inhaling the smoke coming out of the cigarette. It was a nuisance for two strangers passing in front of the shop. They were hiding their noses under the thick muffler. Dave, too, stood at a distance. He was on his phone, looking at some of the daily updates. There was not much going on in his personal life except for this case. There were some calls from his home, but he decided it was better to text them back instead of calling them in the middle of the day. However, one text stood apart from the rest, and Aadi wanted to see him sometime soon. It was work-related. However, he asked him to come without any of his friends and associates. Dave addressed this and set a date to meet the guy. He was in Silver Lake, and reaching him might take a whole day.

"Let's get going?" Blake put off his cigarette.

"Where to?"

"To track the car that you saw outside Rick's place."

"Alright." Dave said with some hesitation. "Let's go then."

Blake looked at him. "Is there a problem?"

"No, but it's just that there are a lot of vehicles in the town and I am not sure that we can track every single one of them."

"Just come. Don't bother yourself with this stuff. I have a plan."

They both entered the car and drove to the town's administration. It was a big old building with a bunch of broken windows. It seemed like a barren place, similar to the ones in the dystopian movies. But there were people inside—working in the different departments.

"Can you elaborate on why we are here?" Dave was not able to restrain his curiosity. He was at a place where he never ever thought to lay his foot.

"I am here to see Jack?"

"Oh, Jack the Ripper, how convenient?"

Blake was in no mood for jokes. "Focus, Dave." He looked furiously in Dave's direction. "Jack is the manager of the transport department. He has a list of all the vehicles registered in the town. Now, he has to shortlist the ones that match your description.

"I get it, detective, but don't you think it's a long stretch?" Dave thought for a second. There are tons of cars that fit my description. Plus, how can you be sure the vehicle belongs to someone living in Pinewood?"

Blake was amazed by Dave's paramount thinking, but they had no choice. "You're right, but it's the best idea I came up with now."

"Alright. Let's get inside."

They both went inside the old building, where sunlight last came 50 years ago. Dave was surprised to see so many people working in the building and to find the place so lively and working. Most employees were sitting on their old desks, and a specific moisturising smell was in the air.

After moving across a couple of rooms in the building, the two were welcomed by a tall figure in a black suit. It was Jack, who was lanky and held a couple of folders in his hand. He had a long, pale face, a tiny nose, and clean-shaven, small hair.

"Officer Blake!" He exclaimed. "Long time and no see."

"Well, it's detective now and secondly you know the town. It's not usually work friendly." Blake replied and shook Jack's hand. He was glad to see him. "Meet my associate Dave."

"Hey Dave."

Dave faked a smile and looked around casually.

"So, what brings you this way?"

"Well, I have a big case on my hands. I just want your help tracking a vehicle."

"A vehicle?"

"Alright. Follow me to my office." He put the folder on an empty desk. The three went to a small cabin with a glass partition. It was congested, and there was not a lot of room to lay three chairs. So, Dave had to stand up during the entire meeting.

"What type of car are you looking for?"

"It's a big black SUV with tainted windows."

Jack waited for a bit. "That's it."

"Yes." Blake replied with a straight face.

"Come on, detective, you need to give me more than that. There are hundreds of black cars in Pinewood. How the hell am I supposed to track the one which you just mentioned with such tiny detail."

Blake looked at Dave. "Is there anything else that you remember?" He put him on the spot, and Dave, who still had some aches from the blow, tried his best to remember the incident. Unfortunately, there was nothing else he could add to the current details.

"I am sorry."

Jack looked at Dave. "Was it new or old?"

"I can't say anything surely but it was not old if you mean the condition. However, I can't say that it was coming straight from the show room."

"Alright. I have to look into some files."

"Thanks Jack. I owe you one."

"No problem, you and Knight saved my ass in the false accusation, a few years back. Its the least I can do."

"Well, we were just doing our jobs."

"Speaking of that, where is Detective Knight these days?"

Blake was stuttering. "You don't know?"

"What?" Jack asked.

"Umm, he passed away six months back."

"My God, I am so sorry; that's sad and tragic." Jack couldn't believe his ears. All his enthusiasm faded within seconds. Meanwhile, Dave had no idea about the person they were talking about. However, he noticed Blake in a few tears after recalling the deceased.

"What happened?"

"Well, he, I—we were working on a case in the northern part of the country. It was a rough case, involving a lot of bad people." Blake paused for a second. "Long story short, he died during a shootout."

"That's so unfortunate. I am glad you're doing ok."

"Leave it." Blake stood from his seat. "Can you work on this and let me know when you're done?"

"Sure." Jack understood that Blake was not comfortable speaking about his dead partner. He left the cabin, and Dave gave Jack his number so he could update him if something came up. The two left the building and moved towards their car. Blake immediately started smoking to calm himself. Dave didn't say much but understood what the detective was going through.

"It might take a couple of days for Jack to come up with something? Don't you think so?"

"Yes, you're right. It might take him more days actually." Blake looked at his cell phone. "Look, it's Friday, I think we should wait for Jack's reports and then work from there."

"Sounds good to me."

"Well, then you're free to leave."

"What?" Dave was a little surprised.

"Yes, you can rest a bit and then if something comes up, I'll contact you. Is that alright?"

Dave thought for a second. "Sure, just be safe."

"You too." Blake put down his half-left cigarette and went into his car. "Do you need a ride home?"

"Nah, I am good." Dave assured the detective that he wanted him to take some time.

"Alright. I'll keep you posted."

He drove away, and now Dave was in front of the old building. He was free for the time and wanted to make the most of it. So, he called Aadi and asked him to meet him in the middle of Pinewood and Silver Lake. There was an old spot on the side of the road between the two towns. Aadi was also free and agreed to see his friend at the destination.

XV
News

The two met at the side of the road. It was above the mainland, and the view from the edge of the roadside was spectacular. Dave rented a bike to reach the place. Meanwhile, Aadi drove all the way from Silver Lake—he arrived first and parked his car on the side of the road. He enjoyed the splendid view while waiting for Dave, who came after ten minutes. He stopped the bike behind the car and placed his helmet on the backseat of his ride.

"How long have you been waiting for me?" Dave asked as he fixed his hair on the one side.

Aadi moved towards his friend. "Nothing, just five minutes." They both shook their hands. "So, how was the drive?" Aadi looked at the motorcycle.

Dave took a long stretch and relaxed his back muscles. "It's been a while since I drove a bike."

"I can see that." Aadi moved to the back of the car and leaned sideways on it. He supported his posture while gazing around. There was not a lot of traffic on the route, considering it was a remote place.

"So, what do you have for me?" Dave asked to focus on the case.

"I wanted to meet you because I saw Simon and Elliot in Silver Lake."

"Really! When?" He was flabbergasted by the news.

"A few days back when you were working with the detective. The place near to my home. They were in a car and meeting someone—it was before your hospitalisation after your incident."

Dave was confused as hell. "So, what happened next? Who was the guy?"

"Well, coming to that-" He took a pause. "I didn't know who the man was, but he seemed a bit old. Well, I thought I would greet them, but they completely ignored me and left before I could reach them."

"Really, and what about the guy?"

"He drove in his own car?"

"Which way did he go?"

"Opposite to your friends."

"Did you see the numberplate of the car?"

"Nah, I am telling you I was quite far and that's why I was moving towards them."

"What car was the man driving?"

"It was a small grey car. One of the common models around Silver Lake."

Dave thought for a second. He was trying to contemplate everything in his brain. Aadi gave him time to think it all through because it was not the only thing he knew.

"One more thing. Mr and Mrs Cooper are selling their house."

"What? Again?"

"Yes, I got this news from a subordinate. He told me that they are planning to leave the country."

"Are you serious?" Dave couldn't believe his ears.

"Why'd you think I asked to meet you in a hurry?"

"It doesn't make sense," Dave murmured. A phone call would have also been nice for a heads-up, but thanks for all this information."

Aadi laughed a bit. "Dave, it's not the news, but I just want you to be aware that you can't trust anyone in this case." He continued. "I mean, the same logic goes for me, but I just want to tell you that something bad is up and you don't want to end up in collateral damage."

"What are you trying to say?"

"The people who call themselves your friends or associates. I don't trust them, and you should, too. They might be involved with people or in certain activities related to the case."

"I get it but I have no other option but to continue on this investigation."

"I respect that but be careful because don't you think that the person who hit you could kill you as well?"

Dave was silent as he looked down the steep hill. The cool breeze numbed his face, and he felt peace. He was waiting for it to end, and it did after a long minute that felt like a second of eternity. He came back to his senses as the image of the missing girl came to mind.

"When will Ella's parents leave?"

"Maybe in a month or so depending on their deal."

"And do you have any idea about their sudden departure?"

"Unfortunately, no." He saw Dave's disappointed face. "But I can figure out something through one of my connections."

"That'd be great."

The conversation fell into an awkward silence as the two stared around the green landscape. To overcome their total stillness, Aadi brought up the detective's name.

"So, where did Blake's investigation reach? And what did you do to help him?"

"Don't start with that. It's pretty difficult, to be honest. Every time we're on to something, an obstacle impedes our progress—back to zero."

"Well, it's like a myth of Sisyphus," Aadi commented while comparing his friend's situation.

"You're talking about that boulder guy?"

"Yes. That's the one."

"So, how can we overcome this situation? Is there an end to all of this?"

"I am certain that there is an end to your mess, but you should not focus on that except for constantly working."

"You're right. Focus on the way through rather than wasting my time thinking about the end." Dave felt a bit motivated. "I want to ask you something." He changed his tone.

"Shoot."

"Who is Officer Knight?"

Aadi was surprised to hear this name. "You mean the detective Knight."

"Yes, that's the name."

"Why'd you ask?"

"Nothing, I heard this name and saw Blake a bit lost in his behaviour."

Aadi started to narrate everything. "Well, Knight was a brilliant detective but last year he was working on a case with Blake. It was a horrendous case that happened in a local town south of the country. Nevertheless, Knight and Blake worked very hard to solve it but unfortunately,

Knight died during investigation. The man who shot him was killed by Blake. It was a rough blow to him as he was never the same without his mentor." He paused. "Well, that's all I know but there could be different reasons for his behaviour. No one can tell."

"How old was the detective?"

"He was around 40. The two worked together for over a decade and they had the best clearance rate in the whole country. Their investigation helped me a lot during the start of my career and I wish things were different. But you know the reality of their jobs—someone will always be present on the other side of the gun. That time, it was Knight."

"You're right." Dave sighed. "Oh man, I should probably leave Blake on his own. The man has been through a lot."

"I bet but I think he needs this case to get back in his life. After losing his job, I think it's the right thing for him."

"I thought he quit." Dave said confusingly.

"No, he was sacked for going against his seniors or so I heard."

"But didn't he solve the case."

Aadi smirked a bit. "It's funny that you can lose your job even after delivering it. I guess following orders is much more important than the task. But hey I don't blame them, it's the way the police forces operate in the region and did for so many years."

"But still, I feel bad for the guy. First, he lost his friend and then his job too."

"Me too but what can we do about it?"

Dave looked at his clock. It was already midday, and he needed to go back to Pinewood. "I should head back. You want to come?" he asked Aadi.

"One day, I'll visit you, when things are better. Right now, you have a lot in your hands and I don't want to get in the way of your investigation."

"Well then, thank you for your information. It means a lot. I'll look into it and see what my friends from the town are up to."

"Yes, coming back to that. Don't let them know it was me. Plus, be careful, I don't think they are working in your best interests."

"I doubt it but I will look into it for sure. I don't want any holes or moles in my work at this time."

"Alright, I'll talk to you later. Drive safely." They both shook hands and went their separate ways. Dave was still thinking about the new information. He needs to talk with Simon. However, he was in the city, so his next move was to meet Elliot and see what he was up to? Also, he needs to be careful about sharing any information regarding the case from now on, as he doesn't know who he can trust. He strapped his riding jacket and put on a helmet. The wind was freezing, and it could be a long and tiring journey back to the town. Dave decided to take some breaks in between as his hands were getting cold. Plus, there was a sort of misty and foggy weather all over the region—making it difficult to see and thus drive.

Even though the distance back to town was roughly two hours, his different intervals made the journey comparatively longer when he drove in the morning. He reached Pinewood around 5, returned his bike, and cared for the business. He then walked to his apartment to rest for a bit. In the meantime, he asked Elliot to meet him in a local bar. He wanted to know about his whereabouts and what was happening with Simon.

After reaching his place, he shut his phone and quickly napped. However, Dave overslept and woke when a light from outside fell directly into his eyes. It was around 8, and he hurriedly grabbed his phone. He saw there were some messages. He primarily focused on Elliot, who was waiting for him at a bar.

Dave was already an hour late, and Elliot was different from the type of person who would wait for him, especially after the situation.

Dave ran rapidly towards the bar. Luckily, it was only a few blocks from his place. He entered the place to find it fully stacked with the locals. He saw Elliot with a drink at the far end of the place. He moved towards and sat beside him. The man was not glad to see him. He looked at Dave and then at his watch.

"What took you so long?"

"I was stuck in the traffic."

"But you don't even have a ride." He looked confused. "Forget it, have a drink and save me some time by vomiting whatever you have in your mind."

Dave asked the bartender for a beer, who acted immediately upon the customer's request. He had no idea how to phrase the situation, but he tried his best.

"Look man, I know things are not good between us and I don't blame you, me or anyone else. It is what it is?" Elliot nodded at his pal. "But I want to ask you something regarding the case?"

"Alright, what is it?"

"I want to know about you and Simon working on something together?"

"Me and Simon?" He chucked. "What do you mean? I haven't seen him for the past two days."

"No, it's before that." Dave hesitated for a bit. "I saw you in Silver Lake meeting with an anonymous guy."

"That bitch journalist!" Elliot was furious. "He told you."

"No, he didn't. I saw you guys."

"Well, you're not a good liar." He stomped on the desk angrily, and people gave him different looks. "I will punch him the next time I see him."

"You won't go near him."

"Oh, yeah, make me." Elliot stood right in front of Dave.

"You don't want to do this." Dave tried to calm his friend down, but he was too drunk to care. He pushed Dave, who fell to the ground. The water was above the bridge, and without thinking for a second, Dave threw a right hand, which landed directly on his friend's chin. He was dizzy for a bit, and then Dave shoved him to the ground—he was unconscious, and the people gathered around. The club had a big scene, and both were escorted out.

Dave took Elliot and let him rest on the side of the street. He knew pushing him was wrong, but he had no other option. He waited for him to get back to his senses. Fortunately, the man was alive and woke up within a few minutes.

Elliot didn't remember much but felt a minor headache. However, upon seeing Dave, he realised what had happened some time ago.

"What the hell is wrong with you?" He said in a blurry tone.

"You attacked me first."

"So, are you going to kill me then?"

"Shut up, Elliot." He gave his hand to lift him up. "You're just drunk."

"I know." He was rubbing his hand and massaging his neck. "So, what do you want from me?"

"Just the truth." Dave said sincerely. "What were you and Simon doing in Silver Lake?"

"Nothing that you need to know."

"Do you want to sleep again?" Dave threatened his friend. "Just answer the damn question!"

Elliot took a deep breath. "Look, we were just there to meet Rob."

"Rob?" The name sounded familiar to Dave. "Is he the same guy who used to sell drugs in college?"

"Yes, Rob, the drugman."

"You are dealing in drugs then." Dave said presumingly.

"No, god, no." He was intimidated by his friend. "Simon wanted to get high and he came to me asking for Rob. I called him to find out that he was in Silver Lake. So, we drove all the way to the town in order to fetch some stuff."

Dave pondered for a bit. "What kind of drugs?"

"I don't remember."

"Really?" Dave was not a bit surprised. "Alright, you can go back. I will deal with this later after getting in touch with Simon."

Elliot swayed and started moving back to his car. He was too drunk to drive. So, Dave decided to help him through. He went before him. "Let me drive you back home." He opened the back door, and Elliot fell on the back seat. Dave carefully seated him and took the car keys from his jacket pocket. He then drove him back to his home. However, he didn't go in since Elliot was drunk, and he might face his parents' endless questions. He gently banged Elliot's face to wake him up and told him to get inside his house. Now, he was free and ready to walk home. He tried reaching Simon to find out about his home predicament, but he didn't respond.

It's been a while since he's been in touch with Simon, and he was getting a bit worried, especially after knowing about the drugs. After trying a couple more times, he decided to take the matter to Blake.

After walking for over twenty minutes, he reached Blake's address. It was pretty dark inside. He rang the bell, but no one responded. It was odd, considering Blake was never out of town without informing. He knocked on the door, and it was opened. Dave was daunted and carefully entered the place without making any noise. He turned the lights on and saw that the place was a mess—more than usual. It was as if some crusade went inside the property. Everything was scattered around, and things were pulled apart. Nothing was in its standard setting. Dave was still trying to reach the detective, but there was no reply. He was worried about him, and he could do nothing now. He needed to find him in case something was terribly wrong with him. He went outside and looked for his car. It was not parked across the street, meaning that he was out, but he could be anywhere, and it was significantly challenging to find someone at this time of the hour. Dave didn't have any ride, but then he realised he mistakenly took Elliot's car keys.

XVI
Nothing Is Everlasting

Dave ran back to Elliot's place. He was out of breath, and the wind was freezing and tiring him faster than the sunny day. Upon reaching Elliot's home, he saw the car, and without thinking for a second, he got inside and drove it away from the locality. Luckily, no one saw him, plus he would probably return it at dawn. Now, the task was to find Blake; he had no idea where to start from? He didn't know him well but was willing to take his chances.

First, he filled the car's tank at the diesel station since it was running low on fuel. After that, he drove through the town, especially around the bars and cafeterias. There was still time for midnight, and many pubs were open.

Dave went through all the open bars to find Blake; he even looked for Blake's car in the parking spaces. Now, it was getting difficult as the areas in the town were receding to look. While driving on an open road, he saw a familiar vehicle. It was Blake's car on the side of the road. It was on the outskirts, and a small road led to the top of the ridge.

Dave parked his car just behind Blake's and kept going on the way. He was a bit scared but had no other option. He reached the top using the flashlight from his phone and some assistance from the moonlight. It was a place similar to where Dave used to go during his tough days. There was a barren railway track on the side. Dave thought it was unusual to find such an old track in Pinewood. It was ancient, rusty and broken. After reaching the edge, he saw a figure sitting on the sidetrack. Finally, Dave was able to locate the detective. He didn't see him until he was standing right next to him.

"Dave, you spooked me." Blake almost reached for his revolver. "What the hell are you doing here?"

"I am looking for you. I searched the entire town but you were nowhere to be seen. Plus, you didn't pick my phone so I was worried for you."

"You shouldn't be. I already told you to rest for a few days. It's been a long and tiring investigation. "You need some rest," Blake said as he drank from an old beer bottle. He was thrashing the place with empty and broken glass bottles. "Come here." He gestured to Dave to sit beside him. "Do you need a drink? I have some beer with me."

"Nah, I am good, I just want you to be ok."

"I am doing just fine," Blake replied strictly. He didn't want anyone to pity him or his condition.

"Listen detective, I know you don't need my help but I just want you to know that losing people is part of life and you can only think of the good parts."

Blake looked around like he didn't hear anything. "You don't know anything. So, just grab a drink or leave me alone."

"Is this about Detective Knight?" Dave continued.

"Look, I am going to ask very politely, get the hell out of here."

Dave didn't move a muscle. "I won't leave you because I know what it's like to stand on the edge and wait for everything to cease to exist. But it's not right away and will never be. So, come with me and let's end what we've started before anyone else gets hurt."

Blake didn't say a word. His eyes were teary, and he sipped the last drop from his bottle. He threw it down the ridge and stood up. He saw the rigid figure of Dave waiting for him to get back on track.

"Let's get going." Dave started following the detective, and they both went towards their cars. No one said anything until they reached their respective vehicles.

"You bought a car! How long have I been up there?"

"Very funny officer." Dave opened the door. "It's Elliot's."

"He gave it to you?"

"Something like that but I have to return it before he knows about it."

"Ok." Blake paused and lit a cigarette. "He lives in town I guess."

"Yes indeed."

"Alright, I'll follow you and you can return it. From there we can go back to our work."

"Sounds good to me."

"Dave entered the car and started driving back to Elliot's. He saw Blake following him through the rearview mirror. He was glad to find him but worried that he was very drunk. Fortunately, they safely reached the town. Dave quietly parked the vehicle on the roadside, just in front of Elliot's house. No one knew that he had taken the car and that he wanted to keep it that way. So, without making any sound, he deliberately returned to Blake's car; the detective was watching and smoking the whole time.

"I can drive if you want." Said Dave as he saw the drunk driver.

"You want to come and sit, or else I leave you here in the dark."

Without any other option, Dave entered the car. He wore his seat belt for the first time in his life. Blake somehow reached his place. He parked the vehicle adjacently, and it was sure to make a scene in the morning. After entering his apartment, Blake realised the mess he'd made before going rouge and drunk.

He looked around. "I have to work on my temper." Blake sighed.

"We all need to in some way."

They scooted into the area and adjusted some of the papers and clothes—just enough to make room for them to sit and talk. Blake was lethargic and needed rest, while Dave was curious about the officer's past.

"Do you need anything? Dave asked the officer to make him sober.

"You are asking as if there's anything in my stupid home."

Dave couldn't argue but went inside the kitchen to look for something useful. He was unsuccessful as there was nothing, or even if there was something, it would have been useless as Blake was asleep on the spot where he sat. It was an hour past midnight, and the town was quiet; everyone except Dave was awake. He decided to return to his place and return in the morning when the detective was in his senses. He responsibly closed the door and went back to his home. He was a bit hungry, but there was no place where he could find food in town. So, with an empty stomach and restless mind, he also tried to get some sleep.

The morning came, and Dave waited all night for the sun to come up before returning to the detective. He got ready and bought some bread for breakfast. When he reached the place, Blake was already awake and having tea. He seemed a bit nauseated, but it was natural for any drunk person.

"You good Detective?"

"Yes, much better than yesterday." Blake stopped his movement and looked at Dave. "Would you like something to eat?"

"Nah, I am good. Just had some breakfast."

"Alright. Suit yourself." He went to his room and seemed pretty normal. When he came back, he was on a call. After a few yeses and noes, he held up and sat before Dave.

"It was Jack from the administration. He has something for us."

"That's great."

"Hmmm, he'll be at his office in an hour or two. We'll visit him there."

"Alright." Dave waited for a second and looked around. The detective noticed the curiosity on his face.

"Is anything troubling you?" He asked and stood in front of him.

"Yes, yesterday, you were drunk to the limit. I just want to know if there is anything I can do for you." Dave took some money out of his wallet. "I know you are struggling, so it's a little help from my end."

Blake saw the money and chucked. "You'll pay when the case is done. I can survive till then. Plus, I'll probably get drunk once again. So, you should have the money." Blake went to his room.

"Alright, it makes sense." He put the money back in his pocket and took a seat. There was still something bothering him, and it was Blake's history. However, he felt ludicrous about discussing someone's past out of context.

Blake came out and showed Dave a small photograph. It was him in a white uniform.

Dave took the photo from his hand and looked at it awkwardly.

"This was my first day on the job. I was 20 years old when I joined the police department." Blake sat in front of him. "I was excited as I was the first officer from my family, and it was a proud moment in my life. The first couple of years were mostly paperwork since there was not a lot of crime in Hilltown. It was the same until I met Detective Knight. He came to the town to retire and live freely. However, a major crime in Hilltown pulled him back to his old ways. He was the best of us and a great police officer. I was assigned to be his partner in the investigation. It was my first case, and after cracking it, we worked on several other cases." He laughed a bit. "It was a great period for us. In 10 years, we solved every case in front of us. We had differences on some occasions, but I respected him, and so did the others." Blake's eyes were getting teary. "Last year, we had a case on our hands. It was the most brutal one that I saw in my entire career. We nearly solved it and were on our way to reach the fugitive. However, someone or somehow, he knew that we were heading towards him. So, he was ready. It was a barren place or a house. I entered from the back. It was dark, and I had to use a flashlight. As soon as I took a few steps, the man started to shoot at me. I immediately took cover, and Knight was on the opposite side. He was entering through the front door. As the bullet rate dropped, I rushed towards the entrance, to escape the scene. However, Knight was already in. I tried to push him out, but it was late as the man already started shooting at me again. Knight hurriedly pulled me out of the house but came before me. He took three bullets to the chest and that was it. The man shot himself after and I was left with the detective. He was unconscious and died at the scene." Dave paused for a bit and looked around. He tried to keep his tears, but it was too much for him. "The man saved me but I didn't do the same for him." He washed his tears. "Later, the backup arrived and everyone wanted answers from me. But I was a coward. I didn't want anyone to know that Knight died while saving me. So, I just made up the story that the culprit shot Knight so in defense, I killed him."

There was silence for a couple of minutes. Dave couldn't believe his ears.

"Why'd you tell me all this?" Dave asked in astonishment.

"Because you're the only one who asked without judgement." He continued. "Everyone wanted to know the details but none of them cared. For them, it was just another day in the office. A man gave his life for this dangerous job and all they cared about was the statistics and numbers. It was getting painful for me to go to work every day. So, I just quit and started working individually so that if anyone gets hurt, it's me."

"Then why did you take me in the case?" Dave looked at him with seriousness.

"Because I thought you might quit in the middle of the investigation. But I was wrong, your love for that girl only makes you fearless and I don't know how to stop you! Because even if I don't help you, you'll be on the streets on your own."

Dave smiled and shook his head in embarrassment. "It's true. Let me ask you one thing, before I came you were already working on Philip's case."

"Yes, it was my obligation to the department to solve the case. It was the least I could do to get them off from my life. But I was wrong again as it was not the case I expected it to be. You came with the different details and now I think we're onto something."

"I suppose." Dave sighed. "But I don't know how long it will take for me to find Ella."

"Dave, if she's alive, then I am pretty sure we'll get to her," Blake said to his partner. Come on, let's meet with Jack and see what he has in store for us."

The two were set to meet Jack at the car administration office. Dave was still trying to reach Simon, but his cell was off. He had not told the detective about Simon and Elliot's little drug adventure in Silver Lake as it would make them both suspicious in his eyes.

The morning time was leaving, and the sun was almost up. It was a bright day in Pinewood, and people were going on with their day. The two investigators reached the administration. Jack was already waiting for them in the parking lot. Maybe he didn't want anyone else to see his association with the police. Or perhaps he wanted to keep all this confidential.

"Detective, how are you?"

"I am good. What's the information?" He jumped right into the topic. Jack didn't even have the opportunity to greet Dave.

"Ok. So I looked for the given details and unfortunately there was no vehicle that matched your description." The two were disappointed upon hearing this news. "However, there is a report of a missing vehicle from a small village, just outside our town. And it matches your description."

"Really, that's great." The detective had a big smile on his face. "Thank you Jack."

"It's my honour to help you, detective. Here," He handed a small file to Blake. "It's the copy of the missing car report and some other details you might need for the investigation. And if you need anything else, you are more than welcome to reach me."

"Thanks, man." They bid farewell to Jack, who rushed hurriedly to his office. Blake opened the file to see the registered details. The vehicle belonged to Kyle, a local restaurant owner of the 'Red Leaf" village, 13 km outside Pinewood Town. It was a pretty small community and not visited very often by anyone. Nonetheless, it was the investigator's next destination, and they didn't want to waste more time.

"Let's go." Dave sat in the car. Blake handed him the file after a few minutes of introspection. He started driving towards the village. He even asked Dave to give a heads-up to Kyle so that they could have a chat with him. Luckily, the man was at his shop. He sold fast food on the side of the fast lanes. They reached his place within half an hour. The shop was in the middle of nowhere, but it had a bunch of vehicles waiting for their food inside the large serving hall.

As they parked their car, a short middle-aged man in middle-aged casual clothing came to their aid. He gestured to stop the vehicle. He had a small cloth in his hand. He was probably cleaning inside his roadside restaurant. That's what Dave thought. He was the first to meet the guy who shook his hand and smiled at him.

The detective also stepped outside and was greeted by the man.

"You must be Kyle," Blake asked as he looked around. "And this must be your shop?

"Yes, officer. It's nice to meet you." He immediately remembered something. "Would like some tea, we can talk inside."

"Yes, sure."

Kyle rushed inside and ordered his worker to make tea for the guests. He even set up a table for them. It was private and away from the casual, monotonous hall where the other guys sat and ate.

"Wait for a bit. I'll be back in a couple of minutes." Kyle left the two at the table. Clearly, the man was busy and had a lot on his hands. However, he came within a few minutes with two hot cups of tea in a beautiful floral patterned tray. He sat adjacent to the two guys.

"Thank you very much," Dave replied, taking a cup from the tray and looking at the man.

"So, how can I help you?" He asked the investigators.

Blake started, "Mr Kyle, I know you're a busy guy, and we won't take much of your time. I already read the details about your missing car, but I want to know the whole incident because I think that someone has abused your car and committed a crime in Pinewood."

"Sure sir, I'll tell you everything." The man took a deep breath and started his story. "So, the robbery took place eight weeks back. It was Saturday night. I came from work and was a bit drunk. I parked the car outside my house. I don't live far from here, but it was a rainy day and some drizzles when I reached home. The next day my car was missing and I immediately thought it was stolen. So, I went to the nearby station to report my case but haven't heard much from them."

"Do you suspect anyone?"

"No sir, I am completely clueless because it was a shock to each and everyone of us in the society."

"Don't you have any CCTVs in the area?" Dave shot one of his own inquiries, which somewhat impressed Blake.

"Unfortunately, no since it was the first robbery which took place in this region."

"I get it but still you might have suspected someone or something odd about that day."

"Nothing that I could remember but there was one thing which always bothered me a lot."

"What was it?"

"It was one week after the incident and I was going to my shop. And all of a sudden a car passed me and I am certain that it was my own car."

"Are you sure?"

"Yes, it was the same model."

"What about the number plate?"

"Well, coming to that, there was no number plate and that's why it made me think that that was my car."

"Where did it go?"

"Well, it was coming from the direction of Silver Lake and maybe going to Pinewood. I don't know, it might have taken a turn in between."

"And did you see who was driving the car?"

"Yes, about that, the car had black tinted windows which was pretty unusual considering it was an offence in the country. So, I didn't see the driver but it was weird to see such a vehicle roaming freely on our streets."

"Did you inform the police of this sighting?"

"I did but you know there was no response from them. I guess they are too busy with other cases."

Blake broke into laughter. "I bet." He paused and looked at Dave, who was looking at his phone. "Alright, I guess that's everything from you, or do you want to tell me something else?"

"I wish but that's all I have for you at the moment but if I ever saw my car again, you'll be the first one on my speed dial."

"I appreciate it. See you around."

Blake left the place while Dave was discussing something with the man. He lit a cigarette and stood at the side of the road. Their suspect was loose and out in the open, and he was probably a dozen steps ahead of them in every possible way.

But one thing still confused Blake, and that was the missing girl. "Where does she fit in all this mess?" he thought as he exhaled the smoke. Dave soon came after and stood beside him.

"Nice man, what do you think?" Dave tried to start the conversation.

"Yup, a very hard working man indeed. What'd you talk about?"

"Nothing, I was just asking him about his work here."

"Alright." He put out his cigarette and threw it on the side of the road. "Let's head back and try to track his car."

They both entered the car and at that moment, Dave received a message on his cell. Simon was returning to Pinewood and would meet him back at his apartment. He was shunned upon seeing the text but was ready to confront his friend on so many things.

The detective asked him about the text, but he refused to disclose any information about the current situation. He wanted to meet his friend first and then decide whether he wanted to share his whereabouts with the detective.

They reached Pinewood, and Dave asked the detective to drop him off at his apartment. Dave thought Blake might be a little suspicious of this, but he didn't even ask a single question about this sudden change of plans. Maybe he had something in mind that he didn't want to share with the rookie.

XVII
Confrontation

Upon returning to his place, Dave saw that Simon stood outside his apartment. He had a carrier bag on his right side and a backpack on his shoulder. He was strolling through his phone, maybe calling Dave and asking for the keys. Luckily, Dave arrived just in time and greeted his lost friend.

"Hey man, where have you been?" He hugged Simon, who had a big smile when he saw his friend.

"I am good; I've been a little busy."

"How is your mother?"

"She's good. She has almost recovered and is back to her normal routine."

"I am glad to hear it." Dave sighed. "What happened to her?"

"Well, she had some sort of rare intestinal infection. It was awful. Took her almost a whole week to recover. And still, after, she got pretty weak."

"The infection was probably very severe."

"You bet."

Dave saw the bags. "Let's get inside. I am sorry to keep you waiting here." He picked up one of his bags after opening the door.

"Help yourself. It might have been a tiring journey."

"It was, but I am good." Simon kept his luggage in the room's corner and sat. Dave brought some soda from the refrigerator and tossed it to his friend.

"Thanks a lot, Dave." He cracked open the can, and it was chilled. Dave sat across from him while analysing his friend. He had many questions, but he decided to give the man a minute to enjoy his soft drink of choice.

"So, what's happening in the case?" Simon asked after a couple of sips.

"Well, there's been another murder, and we don't have any major progress."

"Really." Simon freaked out a bit as he realised something. "Oh crap, I've heard that you've been at the hospital. Someone attacked you during the investigation?"

"Yes, it's true."

"Thank God you're safe."

"Maybe I got lucky, but yes, it was close. Unfortunately, I got the man killed."

"No, man, you can't think like that. It's not good for you!" He continued. "You should be grateful that you are safe, as it would've been disastrous for all of us."

"Maybe you're right." Dave nodded positively. "So. what brings you here?"

"I am sorry?" Simon couldn't believe his ears.

"Why are you here, Simon?" Dave got serious. "What do you want? You should be at home with your family. Why risk your life here, or do you have any other plans?"

"Dave, what the hell are you talking about? I am here because you might need my help."

"Oh, don't give me this excuse. I am not a fool. Clearly, you're here for something else. Tell me, what are you hiding?" Dave said in a loud tone.

Simon couldn't understand the situation. "Dave, I just want to help and keep you safe."

"Oh really, how can you keep me safe? By doing drugs with Elliot!"

Simon realised Dave's anger and leaned sideways, relaxing on the side cushion. "Aadi told you our secret."

"So you were looking for drugs in the middle of the investigation."

"I am sorry, man, but I was in distress and had no other option."

"Don't make such useless excuses," Dave replied immediately. "I know you very well. You're not here to help me but to enjoy the miserable drugs."

"Come on, Dave, it was just a one-time thing. I am an idiot who forced Elliot into this as well."

"I see that, but I am not worried about drugs."

"What do you mean?" Simon was confused.

"I suspect you might have something to do with this case?"

"Are you out of your mind?" Simon couldn't believe his ears. His best friend did not trust him plus accused him of a superficial crime. "I get it. You think you're a great detective, but I must tell you one thing, you are a novice and a fool. I helped you all this time, and you're suspecting me of your stupid crime theories." He stood up. "That's it, I am out." Simon took all his stuff out of the apartment. Dave was watching all this but dared to question his friend again. He was trying to see through him. Simon finally left while his drink lay on the table, and Dave was alone.

After 15 minutes, he received a call from his mother. It had been a while since he picked up her phone. He felt it was the right time to tell her everything he was going through. However, little did he know, she already knew everything happening with her son. It was Simon, he called his family and told them everything that happened in the past.

Dave was not furious; he knew that his lies would come out of the dark someday, and now it was his time to face the judgment of his loved ones.

He didn't say much except replying 'yes' to a couple of questions. He had broken his family's trust, and it might take some time for them to understand his perspective regarding the whole subject. After 15 minutes of objurgation, he was free from the trouble. However, his parents decided not to help him financially until he came home safely. It was sad news to Blake since he was the one who required the money for the investigation.

Dave still had some money, which he could use for a week or two, but after that, he might have no other option but to borrow from someone. Otherwise, he would have to stop working on the case.

Dave had no idea where Simon went, but he didn't care much about his friend then. He was suspicious, but he still had much bigger problems.

He went to Blake's to proceed with the case. Blake was trying to get footage of the vehicle using different data sources. His reputation immensely helped him during the case since many people knew him and owed him different favours. Dave reached his place and saw Blake taking some calls. He gestured to him to wait for a minute. He took his seat and opened some articles on his phone. After a few minutes, Blake hung up and stood before Dave.

"How is your friend?"

"You know about him?" Dave asked surprisingly.

"Yes, I saw him enter your place when I dropped you."

"Really, he told me he was there for a bit." Dave sighed. "Forget it; he's not my problem anymore."

"You should be thankful for that because I don't think he was acting in your best interest." Blake tried to console his partner.

"Maybe I don't know. I mean, he helped to get out of that police station, but he and Elliot were doing drugs behind my back in the name of investigation. And I can't allow that kind of trouble in this case."

"Let him be, but this doesn't mean you can't befriend him. Give him and yourself some time. Things will go back as they were— we have to focus on our work."

"You're right." Dave took a breath. "So, what are you working on?"

"Nothing, just looking at some of the footage from the cameras in the town."

"What? Do you have permission to do this type of stuff? I mean, it's very authoritative and privacy invading."

"Don't worry. These are videos that I got from my contacts. They know I am working on a case, so none of them have declined my situation."

"Ok." Dave continued. "Did you have any success with this stuff?"

"No, not at the moment, but these tons of data will take more than two or three days to get through everything. Plus, some cameras have terrible quality, making it quite difficult to distinguish between the regular and suspected car."

"Don't worry, just give me half of the files. I'll look into it as well." Dave said but was a bit confused. "However, I need a system for this. Do you have a spare laptop?"

"I can arrange something for you until then. Use my computer," Blake replied, and he started looking for something inside his room. Meanwhile, Dave started going through the different files on the computer. There were hundreds of folders with dozens of videos. They were from the street side, behind houses and markets.

"How'd you even gather all this stuff in such a short duration?" Dave was flabbergasted as he scrolled through the information.

The detective came out of his room. He had a small laptop in his left hand. "Well, you will learn about all this stuff when the time comes. For now, you go through the videos. And I'll set up your laptop, which you can use later."

Dave went back to the videos and played the footage at maximum speed. His target was to cover the areas attached to the main street. Because the chances of finding their vehicle were pretty high in those areas.

An hour passed. Dave was still looking at the footage; he didn't have any success, and he expected it. It was going to be a long process before reaching their target.

Blake had already set up another system for Dave, but he gave him some time on his computer. He was looking for some other CCTV sources in Pinewood. It was getting late, but there were still plenty of suspicious areas in Blake's eyes. He had already contacted most of his connections, and everyone cooperated with him.

Dave was getting tired; it's been another two hours since he's been on that computer. Now, he wanted some rest. So he asked the detective to give him his laptop so that he could work on it from his place. He took the computer with the data to his apartment, and upon reaching, he set everything on a small dining table.

However, Dave's eyes were red and tired, and he needed some sleep. After the setup, he went to his room and lay on the bed. He was still thinking about Simon and how he behaved with his friend. But now, there was no point in feeling as it was all in the past. With all these different thoughts in mind, Dave fell asleep.

After sleeping for the rest of the day, he finally looked around. His head was still aching, and he was still half asleep. He looked at his clock. It was midnight, and he was hungry. However, there was nothing to eat. He then checked his phone to see if there was any update from the detective. There was nothing from Blake, so he decided to go outside to find some food.

There were some shops which were open at night. It was cold, so Dave thought of getting some soup. He put on his long coat and left the apartment. There were very few people on the main street of Pinewood. Most of them were drunk or going to get drunk. He reached a place that was selling some noodles and soup.

There was a young boy who was doing the dishes. He ordered some food and stood at the side. Some guys came behind and gave their orders. After 15 minutes, his food was all set, and he took it to sit on a nearby bench. It was cold, but the hot food really complimented the entire situation.

Dave finished his soup and looked at his phone. It was Blake; he was asking for some updates, and Dave had none. He felt guilty to sleep for so long without continuing his work. He decided to ignore the text and enjoy his late-night dinner. However, he decided to go back and continue the work. He was refreshed and complete and could work the whole night til morning on the case.

He went back and, on his way, saw Elliot and Simon. They were entering a local pub. Maybe they saw him, and if that was the case, they completely ignored him. It was apparent that none of them wanted to see his face, and he accepted it.

Dave was a mean and self-centred guy who obliterated all his friendship over some delusion. Now, it was his duty to prove them wrong and find the solution to all this trouble. He came to the front of the pub but refused to enter it and moved along the way. He reached his apartment, hung his coat and sat on the desk.

He started looking through the footage. Time passed, and the sun was around the corner. Dave had his third cup of coffee. He was almost done, and still, there was nothing. He nearly gave up; however, in one of the footage from the west side of the town, he saw the car. It was a black car with tinted windows, without a number plate. He got his phone and hurriedly called the detective to give him a heads-up. He edited that clip, closed his laptop and rushed to Blake's.

There was some fog in the morning, which was comparatively colder than at night. Dave ran all the way to reach faster. He entered Blake's place; he was asleep on the couch. He woke him up even though it was a bad idea.

"Dave, what happened?"

"I got our guy." He took the laptop out of a small backpack. "It was footage from last Wednesday." Blake immediately woke up, rubbed his eyes and took the computer from Dave. He saw the footage. It was from a gas station on the west side of Pinewood. The car was going to the outskirts, near the dense forest.

"Good job, Dave." He stood up. "Give me five minutes to get ready. Let's see where the trail leads us."

Blake was ready. The two left for the forest on the outskirts. It was a dense area, and hardly anyone visited it. Evidently, a culprit could hide or shelter in the forest since no one came. It was around 5 km from the main town.

They reached the petrol station and saw the CCTV, which had captured the car at the same angle a few days ago.

Blake's old friend owned that station but was not present there. He decided to meet him after searching for the vehicle in the entire area. They entered the forest, and Blake slowed his car down to get a better view of the area.

He drove the car as far as it could reach. Once they reached the middle of the place, it was time to continue the journey on foot. The two got out and started moving on a small trail, resembling a trek in the middle of the jungle. It's been half an hour, and there was no sign of anyone or anything.

Everything was green or yellow; the forest was dense compared to the entrance, and it was only the beginning. Dave had lost his sense of direction and was following the detective, who seemed quite capable of finding his way through the woods.

"Detective, where the hell are we going?"

"Just keep moving; it's not that far," Blake replied vaguely.

"What is not that far?" Dave was pretty annoyed about getting hit with a branch in his face. "Are we still looking for the car?"

"Yes. There's an open area in the middle. We are heading towards there."

"But how can a vehicle reach that far inside?"

"First, let's find that car. These questions are for later."

An hour passed, and the two reached an open area similar to Blake's description. It was in the middle, with some open patches free from long grass. It was an open field similar to a picnic ground. However, no one was there, and there were no signs of a vehicle.

"Follow me," Blake commanded as he again took the lead.

"Now, where are we going?"

"Just follow me."

Blake took Dave down the hill into the forest on the other side of the field. They were walking through, and it was getting pretty humid. Then suddenly, Blake stopped. Blake focused on his partner, who stumbled right behind him.

"What?"

"Just keep it down." Blake pointed towards something. "Look, that's our prize."

Dave saw the black, missing car stranded in the middle of nowhere. It was in pretty bad condition, but it was the key to the case. Blake slowly moved across the vehicle. He made sure that they were the only ones there. Upon reaching the car, he carefully started investigating the entire scene.

He asked Dave to call the forensic team to do a thorough investigation. However, there was no reception at their location. So, Dave climbed up the valley and reached a higher point to make the call. He called in the backup, and now it was up to the forensic team to find the clues.

He came down and sat with Blake, smoking on the side of the car. He was relieved to find such a big break in the case. Now, all he needs to do is track down the man behind all this and ensure the case gets closed.

"Pretty clever suspect, don't you think? He made all this effort to leave the car in the middle of this place."

"Yes, but I have seen worse," Blake replied calmly.

"But how did he reach this place?" Dave sat beside Blake. "How can you drive through all this forest in between?"

"There's a road on the opposite side. He might have taken that route; the one we took to reach here is on foot."

Dave was dazzled. "So, you're telling me that there is a way for vehicles to reach directly here."

"Yes." Blake threw his cigarette.

"Then why didn't we take that to get here. It could've saved us three hours."

"I don't know that the car is on this side. He'd probably leave it on the outskirts, but it doesn't matter. We found it, and now this car will lead to our man."

Dave nodded but didn't say anything. He lay on his back to watch the clear skies. The backup and forensic team arrived at the scene after two hours. They were friends with Blake, who explained everything to them. Now, the two were ready to leave the scene. The forensic guys will investigate the area and send them the reports.

Dave was upset that he had to walk again to reach the car. But he had no other option. It was getting dark, and the two finally reached their vehicle. Blake sat and relaxed for a bit. He didn't say much on the way back. Dave was exhausted, too; he needed food and water, and Blake knew the right place. He drove a mile back to his friend at the gas station. He wanted to appreciate his help, but Wiley was not at the shop. Regardless, they ordered some food and coffee.

"So, when will the reports come?" Dave asked with curiosity.

"Maybe one or two days. But not more than that, but let's see. I am not the one in charge. So, I just have to wait like everyone else."

"I get it." Dave was pretty exhausted, but one thing still lingered in his mind. Blake noticed the concern.

"What are you thinking about?"

"Nothing, it's just a thought." Dave dismissed the question.

"You're thinking about Ella."

Dave sighed. "Yes, I don't know, but I feel bad about all this."

"Don't worry. Our job is to seek truth and get justice to the victims. Once you accept that, nothing can break you. You understand?"

"Yes, sir."

"Good, let's get you home. Get some rest, and I'll see you tomorrow. Maybe after receiving the forensic reports."

"What will you do?"

"I'll drop you off and maybe assist the forensic team with the evidence."

"I can also help you."

"No, Dave, you've already done enough. Rest for a while and be ready. Our work is not over yet. Our guy is still out there, and I can't ease until he's behind bars."

"Ok." Dave didn't say much. His body needed rest even though his mind was restless. Blake dropped him back to his place and left. However, Dave didn't want to lay low. He waited for Blake to leave the province, then came outside to walk down the street.

Dave wanted to proceed with the investigation independently and started heading outside. He called Aadi and told him everything about the situation. As he strolled through the streets, he crashed into someone who handed him a piece of paper and ran off.

Dave had no idea; it was so quick that he couldn't even react. He saw the shadow of the man disappearing into the dark alley. Now, he saw the message in his hand. It read: "Light Palace at midnight."

Dave thought it was probably a prank, but it was getting dark. He wanted to tell the detective about this but would have to tell him the truth. In hopes of keeping a clean slate, Dave decided to go alone and see who was asking for him.

XVIII
Light Palace At Midnight

Light Palace was an abandoned place located in the heart of Pinewood. However, no one visited it because it was all dull and rusty. Plus, the government didn't want anyone to be there because of the renovation project.

But still, plenty of drug addicts visited the place for their illegal activities. Dave reached the place by walking directly after the message.

It was not yet midnight, so he decided to wait at the corner of the place. It was better to be early and know about the situation than to be late and not able to tell anything about it to anyone.

He waited more than four hours; it was pitch dark, and the temperature was pretty low. Dave's patience was tested as he was shivering due to the cold. He almost left the place several times, but his conscience thought otherwise. He even thought of calling someone in case of emergencies, but it might have made the situation unfavourable for him.

After waiting for five hours, he saw someone standing at the entrance. The man entered; he wore an oversized coat and a hood inside. His face was not visible. He lifted his head and unveiled himself. He was a young guy with patches of beard, long hair and pale skin. He was not much older than Dave, and his attire didn't resemble a gentleman. Dave was ready for any physical combat. He had a knife carefully placed in his sleeve. It was only time before things could turn dark for them.

"Who the hell are you?" Dave asked to have some dominance over the tall and lean figure.

"You're with the Detective?"

"Yes," Dave repeated once again. "Answer my question!"

"I am Rob. You might have heard about me."

"You're the drug dealer. My friend told me about you."

"Yes, and I don't pose any threat, so you can take that knife out and put it safely in your pocket."

"You think you're smart."

"No, I am just here to talk to you." He said calmly.

Dave was getting comfortable. "About what?"

"The murders."

"Why do you think I am interested in talking when I could just arrest you."

"Look, I know everything about you; you're a rookie" He paused for a bit. "You're not even a real policeman. I am not scared of you. Plus, you would have come with backup if you wanted me to be arrested. You can't take me down, and I am in no mood to be a bad guy in your story. I just want to have a word with you."

Dave looked around and moved towards the man. "Alright. What is it?"

"The car that you found today, I left it in the forest."

Dave was intimidated; he maintained a distance from the man and took out his knife. "You're a murderer."

"See, now you're making this difficult for me."

"So, let's finish this."

The man put his hand in the coat and brought a small pistol. "I can shoot you here right now; no one will ever know. You think I am the bad guy, more power to you, but I didn't murder those people. Just listen to me for one second."

"You have two minutes before I call the Detective."

"Thanks." Rob was glad to hear this. "Listen, I might have my hands in a dirty business, and you're right to judge me, but the car you found is stolen."

"Yes, by you."

"No, I found it at my place. So, I stole it."

"Really! Good, reasonable points by you!"

"I have no idea."

Dave couldn't believe his ears. "And why should I believe this?"

"Because it's the truth." Rob continued. "My fingerprints are in that car; everyone will figure out it was me. I indeed drove that car there, but it doesn't prove that I am a murderer. You have to trust me, I am innocent, and you're the only one who believes me."

"Why do you think that?"

"Because you're the only one who is after the girl?"

"Say that again." Dave was pretty confused.

"Yes, I know about you. Why are you here? You're looking for that girl that disappeared one year ago."

"What do you know about her?"

"Nothing, but you're not the only one who has seen her roaming on these streets."

Dave was flabbergasted. "You have seen her too?"

"Not me, but I know someone."

"Who?"

"I can't tell you his name right now. I first need your assurance to save me in this case."

"Why do I believe you?"

"Because if I am prosecuted in this case, then there is no chance you'll ever know about the girl. Everyone will move on, and this case will be closed. So, please help me, and I'll tell you everything I know about her."

Dave was confused; he was thinking a lot of things, and it was hard to answer the question at the moment.

"Alright. I'll talk to somebody." He agreed with the proposition, and Rob was happy to hear about it. But he was unsure how this news would play in the long run. He went to talk with Blake, who was supposedly working with the forensic team.

He called him on his cell, but unfortunately, the man was very busy with something and was not available to meet. Dave was getting bombarded with different thoughts and scenarios; he wanted to trust Rob, but then again, the man was a thief and drug dealer, and who knows if he was telling the truth? People like Rob are pathological liars.

The night passed, and Dave returned to his apartment after the call. He was set to meet Blake and tell him everything that happened the day before. He went to Blake's apartment. Fortunately, the man was there this time, working on the case. He was surprised to see the young man so early in the morning.

Dave sat in front of the detective and started to narrate everything that happened last night. Blake couldn't believe his ears, and his body language suggested that he was very pissed at Dave. He didn't say much but left his place and started moving back and forth. Dave had no idea what would happen next, nor did he anticipate such a reaction from Blake.

"You let him go?" Blake broke the silence.

"Well, I couldn't catch him. The man had a gun."

"And that's made you believe that he was innocent."

"No, but why else would he come to me?" Dave sounded confused. "He needs our help."

"No," Blake said angrily. "He needs to be behind bars." Dave tried to interrupt the detective but was cut in between. "Let me tell you something, Dave. Criminals are experts in deceiving the innocent because they think they are similar to normal people. But they're not, and it's one of the oldest tricks in their book or code. They'll pursue you to help in something and then leave you stranded while escaping from the case. So, it's the last time I say we'll arrest Rob as soon as his fingerprints are confirmed on the car. And that's that. You can think whatever you want, but it's the right call."

"But what about Ella?"

"Oh god, forget her. She's not real." Blake finally said it. There was silence in the room. Dave was upset and didn't reply. He took his coat and left the place. It was a pretty bad hit from his partner.

Blake realised his mistake, but it was too late, and the man was on his way back. It was sure that there was no way to continue with the investigation. The department will arrest Rob, and the case will be closed. And even if all this goes to the court, it might take years before anything happens.

Dave was at the same place where he had started and could do nothing. However, he thought Rob was not guilty, so he found the man and alerted him of the upcoming events. He didn't have his number but knew he was watching him from somewhere. So, he returned to the Light Palace and met the man. Upon reaching him, to his surprise, Rob was already there and eagerly waiting for him.

Dave didn't expect him to be there. "What are you doing here?" Then he realised. "You followed me to my home and then the Detective's."

"Probably, but that's none of your business. I want to know what the detective has to say?"

"Well. You're going to jail. He refused even to acknowledge your story. Today, when the forensic reports come, the whole police will be after you. I just came to give you a heads-up."

"Oh, god, why? You didn't persuade him enough."

"Just leave it. Don't you think I want to know about Ella? But now there's nothing I can do for you. However, I'll be in debt if you still want to tell me about her."

"No, we made a deal. You should have kept your end of the bargain." Rob didn't show any emotion.

Rob left the place immediately. He was on the run, as it was only a matter of time before the police were on his tail. Dave had no option but to see the man leave in some hope of saving his life.

He didn't want anything else to do with the case. He transferred his remaining money to Blake and wiped the slate clean of his troubles. He returned to his apartment and started packing his stuff; he even informed his landlord that he'd leave his place by the end of the month.

He sat sadly on his couch, waiting for something to happen. It's been a while since he saw Ella; maybe she was an illusion, or he was going insane. Whatever the matter was, it was beyond his comprehension. The day passed, and Dave didn't move an inch as he lay on his couch.

He moved when there was a buzz on his phone. It was Aadi; he was in Pinewood and wanted to see Dave. It was urgent, but Dave was demoralised, so he asked Aadi to come to his place as he didn't want to go out.

Half an hour passed, and Aadi reached Dave's location. He was in a hurry and sat in front of Dave.

"What the hell are you doing here?" Dave asked in a low voice.

"I was in town for some news. You caught him."

"Did the forensic report come?"

"Yes, it's all in the news. He's the guy I told you about! Are you living under a rock?"

"No, I knew about this. I was resting for a bit."

Aadi noticed Dave's low mood. And somehow, he understood the reason behind it.

"You didn't find her," Aadi said in a low voice. Dave knew that it was coming.

"Aadi, let me ask you one thing."

"Yes, go ahead."

"When I said I saw Ella, did you believe me? Be honest for the sake of our friendship."

Aadi was silent for a few seconds. He took a deep breath and continued. "No, I don't." Dave rolled his eyes back. "But that doesn't mean it's not possible. I mean, she could be well and alive, and maybe it was a coincidence that you saw her."

"No, it's not a coincidence; it's not that I stumbled upon her in a coffee shop or something. I saw her at different places abnormally. Maybe there is something wrong with me here." He pointed towards his head.

"Don't say that. You're not ill. We all get confused sometimes."

"Probably."

The two sat opposite one another, waiting for words to disrupt the silence in the room.

"So, what will you do now?" Aadi tried to change a bit of the room's atmosphere.

"I am going back."

"Really?"

"Yes, I'll probably return to the city and pick up where I left."

"So you'll just leave this case here."

"Do you think I have a choice?" Dave said in an angry tone. "I don't have anything here, plus I am broke after paying the detective. And that did a lot for me." He remarked and sighed.

"But I have some new information for you." Aadi came straight to the topic. "The Coopers left the town."

"What?" Dave was surprised. "Already, but you said it might take some time."

"Well, apparently, they got a deal that exceeded their expectations."

"Really, who was it?"

"I don't know him, but she's a local business owner. I'll let you know if I learn anything else."

"Nah, there's no need. I am good for nothing and don't want any further involvement."

"I see." Aaadi looked around. "So, did you meet Rob before his arrest?"

"Yes, he came with a proposition," Dave replied.

"Really, what did he want?"

"Well, he told me he was innocent, and someone left the car on his doorstep. Later, he realised that it was involved in murder, so he left it in the jungle." He continued. "He also knew about Ella and told me he knew someone who might help me find her. But I need to save him in case."

"Did you believe him?"

"Yes, but when I went to Blake with this story, he immediately refused to play any part, which is understandable."

"And what about the guy who left the car with Rob?"

"He didn't tell me anything about him. Maybe the police will extract the truth from him after breaking a couple of bones."

"But if Rob's right, the man who left the car is the real killer."

"He had to be, but the thing is, the police want to solve this case because of all sorts of pressure. And if they have enough evidence and a sacrificial lamb, they'll be happy to put Rob in prison or even worse."

"But that's wrong," Aadi shouted. He was getting frustrated about learning this. He was a reporter, and his work involved objectivity, something clearly missing from the investigation. "You need to convince Blake before it's too late, as you might have the wrong guy in your hands."

"Don't you think I tried? But as I said before, that ship has already sailed, and there's nothing I could do."

"Then ask Rob about the man. If he's real, why would he hide his name and go to jail instead."

"He won't budge.

"Then make him, Dave. Look, you're the only one who cares about Ella. And maybe searching for her is the key to this case. Two people are dead, and one innocent man might get imprisoned for the crimes he never did!"

"He's not that innocent. He sold the drugs to Simon and Elliot."

"But that's far from murder." Aadi was trying his best to convince Dave. "Do I think he deserves some correction in jail? Of course, but not on murder charges. So, I think you have to talk to somebody before it gets more dynamic in the judicial system."

"And what if he's lying? Then I'll be a laughing stock again in everyone's eyes."

"You don't come all this way just to be a bit afraid of being mocked. You loved Ella; it might be your last opportunity to solve her mystery. And I think you need that to keep your sanity."

Dave was speechless. Aadi made a lot of sense, but he needed Blake to do something because he had all the connections and recognition in Pinewood Town.

"I must leave now as I have to cover this case. I hope you find your way around all this." Aadi stood and shook hands with Dave.

"Alright, I'll see what I can do?"

Aadi left, and now it was Dave and his thoughts. He wanted to do the right thing, but it seemed as if all doors had been shut. He tried one last time to contact Blake, but his phone was busy. Maybe he was tangled in delivering the details regarding the case.

It didn't make much sense for him to wait in his apartment. He took his coat and went on the road. As soon as he set foot, he saw Blake on his doorstep.

"Detective, you are here? I was coming to meet you?"

"Dave, I got your message and spoke with Rob upon his arrest." He moved aside, and behind him, Rob stood in disguise. Dave was flabbergasted upon seeing the man.

"What the hell is he doing here?"

"I don't have time for all this. Can we come in!"

The two entered the apartment, and Dave had so many questions.

XIX

A Man Who Knew A Man

"Detective! What is wrong with you? Why did you bring him here?"

"Look, Dave, I don't have time for explanations. I only have around twenty minutes. So, let's do our job for the sake of this investigation."

Rob had a smirk on his face. He knew everything that was happening and was having a great time.

Blake asked Rob to take a seat. The man was in handcuffs. Dave went to the balcony and saw a couple of police officers outside on the street. Their car was also there, meaning it was happening. Blake brought Rob to Dave's apartment for some unofficial questioning.

"Detective, why are you wasting your time? Everyone wants to prosecute me. So, let them. You do not need to step in and save my life." Rob said hysterically.

"Don't try to act like a saint. You're a thief and drug dealer. No one is denying that, but you're probably not the murderer. So, let us help you like you wanted."

Dave stood in front of them. "Detective, what are you thinking here?"

Blake pulled Dave to the other side of the door so Rob could not hear the two discuss.

"Listen, this might not be our guy, and I don't want him behind bars knowing that the real suspect might still be out there." Dave nodded, agreeing with the detective. "However, we have to assure him he'll be safe because that's the only way to make him talk."

"But do you think that he's right?" Dave asked in confusion. "You were quite sceptical of him the night before."

"I was, but then I looked into the pieces, and there were still some holes left, which made zero sense. Also, I had a word with him before his arrest. I thought he might hide, run, or leave this town, but he came right to me."

"What did he say to you?"

"Nothing. He had the same story, but he revealed one name, and maybe it's best for you to hear from him."

The two returned to Rob, who was looking out the window at the back of the street.

"So, Detective, you told him about that man?" Rob asked sarcastically.

"No, I didn't. Tell him what you know about the missing girl." The detective ordered the guy.

"You like to play tough, don't you?" He laughed. "Anyway, I am going to jail, so screw it." He looked at Dave. "Look, kid, I don't know you, but you seem like a nice guy. Plus, maybe you can set me free from these accusations. So, here it goes." Rob started with the story. It was surprising for Dave that the man was ready to talk. Maybe the fear of injustice is more than the fairness of justice.

"Six months ago, I had to deliver some weed to a local man in Silver Lake. It was getting late, and it was my last gig. I reached the place and found the man. He was a doctor named Gary."

Dave couldn't believe his ears. "You mean Gary Wise?"

"Yes, that bum. You know him?"

"Yes. He filed a police complaint against me during the early part of the investigation. Why did he need drugs?"

"To make Sushi!" Rob replied sarcastically and looked at Blake. "Where did you get this guy?" He shook his head in disappointment. "Anyway, he was on the phone with someone. However, the area was dead silent. I could hear the other end of the phone line. And as I was handing him his package, I heard a scream on the phone; it was a girl, and she was asking for help."

"What did she say or sound?"

"She said, 'Let me out of here!' It was a brutal and frightening sound. At first, I tried to ignore that sound, but the doctor realised it was audible. He immediately hung up and paid me. He ran towards his car and left the place. It was a pretty odd thing to happen, but I ignored it because of how the hell I was supposed to talk with someone regarding such matters. I am a criminal, and my word is as good as a house of cards, so you can understand me."

Dave had so many questions in his mind, and he was furious. At that moment, if Gary was in front of him, he might have killed him. But he tried to calm himself with reason.

"How'd you know it was Ella or not some other girl?" Dave asked confusingly.

"I am not certain, but you tell me how many girls have disappeared from this region. I can bet it was the girl you're searching for."

He heard everything that Rob had to offer. Now, it was time to proceed with the case.

"Thanks, Rob, if this is true. I will make sure to free you as soon as possible."

"Don't worry, kid, I probably deserve some time in jail, but I believe you can get the real man behind all this mess."

Dave looked at Blake, who stood there the entire time. He ran out of time and took Rob to the police department.

"I'll catch up with you later," Blake said as he left the apartment.

Dave had a feeling from the start that Gary Wise had something to do with the case, and now he had evidence against him.

This time, he can visit the man with official assistance and find the truth behind the mystery. He knew that Ella's parents left the town because they were hiding something. It was the same reason that they left Pinewood in the first place.

Now, all Dave has to do is wait for Blake after he returns from the police department. Also, they don't have much time as Rob might face much trouble from the police department. Blake delivered the man to the police. Therefore, his role was over since the officers would take care of the evidence and press conferences in the town.

Blake returned to Dave, who was articulating several reasons to not murder Gary Wise. He didn't like the guy, but he needed to be calm and collected.

"So, when are you planning to leave?" Dave asked Blake, who was looking at something on his phone.

"Soon, let me sort some things out, and we'll be on our way to this guy."

"Ok."

They both drove to Silver Lake Town to visit Gary Wise. None of them spoke much about the case except that Dave wanted to know more about his man.

"Did Rob tell you about the guy who left the car with him?"

"Nah, he had no idea about the vehicle or the man who abandoned it. However, for some reason, it was evident that they knew the kind of man Rob was. So they decided to leave the car to him."

"He's a smart man." Dave was pretty impressed. With that, he got lost in the scenes of the way and even fell asleep. They both reached Silver Lake Town.

They found that Gary was at work after calling his office. Plenty of patients were in the hospital, but it didn't matter to either of them. They stormed through the crowd and entered Gary's cabin. He was not occupied with anything and was on a call. He immediately recognised Dave and was a bit frightened.

"What the hell are you doing here?" Gary tried to intimidate the two men. "Get out, or I'll call the police."

Blake tried to act as the intermediary between the two souls. "Doctor Gary, I am Detective Blake, and he's with me, so please cooperate. We're here for a few questions if you don't mind."

The doctor looked at him. "I am not at liberty to answer your questions."

"You are because we are in the middle of a criminal investigation, and you're not allowing us to do the police work."

Gary couldn't believe his ears. "What the hell do you mean by that? I am here working on helping the patients, and you are making my workspace chaotic. So, please leave."

"We'll leave after you answer our damn questions."

"I don't think I will."

Blake smirked and looked at Dave standing just by the door. He understood the assignment and pulled the curtains so no one could see inside.

In one instance, Blake smacked the tooth out of Gary's mouth. It was brutal and effective as it broke the man. He started crying, and even the painful words took a toll on his mouth.

"Now, I am asking again. Where is Ella?"

"I don't know."

"What do you mean you don't know?" Blake asked seriously. "I have a genuine source who has heard her on your cell phone. And don't forget about your drug use. I know everything about you? So please help us so that we might save you from prosecution. Where are you hiding her?"

"I am not." Gary held his face with his left arm. "She ran away."

"Enlighten me."

The two sat in front of Gary, who was scared for his life at the moment. He has never felt intimidated like this in his life. And with such pressure, he was broken and collapsed into small pieces.

"Alright. Let me explain."

"Good." They both took their seats.

"So, you probably know that Ella had a heart condition, and she had less than one year to live. I have a good relationship with the Cooper family. One day, Mr Cooper came to me about this situation. He was a broken man, and I wanted to help him, but our options were limited. A heart transplant was our only option. But for that, you need a donor, plus there are a hundred complications in the procedure. However, I knew some of the best doctors and surgeons who might have pulled this off." He took a deep breath. "But there was one major problem, and it was still the donor. Pinewood is small, and hardly any donors share Ella's genetic structure. So, we had no other option but to reach the city's black markets. Some big hospitals harvest organs, which you can get for the operation. But that cost too much, and the Cooper family didn't have that much money."

"So, what did they do?"

"They were still making assumptions, plans or strategies, but none made sense."

"Ella knew that this was happening?"

"No."

"How can you say that?" Dave asked with curiosity.

"Because I met her one day and discussed her condition." He continued. "She had already accepted her fate and had no hope for the future. I tried to give her hope, but that ship had already sailed. I wish her parents understood that."

"What do you mean?"

"So after months of disappointment, time was running out, and I know that they were seeking external help, but this was madness."

"What are you talking about?"

"The Coopers somehow found an individual that could be a donor for Ella."

"That seems like a good thing." Dave intervened.

The doctor looked at Blake. "You're both are so naive. You should do some other job."

"What?" Dave was startled.

"You don't understand; the individual was only 15 years old and not a donor. Mr Cooper planned to forcefully transplant the heart after killing the young man."

"That's why they kidnapped her. She was in the town the entire time." Blake was shocked. "Where did they find this man?"

"You have to ask Mr Cooper about this?"

"Mr Cooper?" Dave asked in surprise.

"Yes, he was the one who found the man."

"Who was this man? The guy who got murdered?"

"I don't know, but he could be. I don't know that much."

"When did Ella call you?"

"It was a few months back. I didn't expect it at all, but somehow, she found a way to reach me. It was right in the middle of my interaction with that junkie."

"And you alerted her family!" Dave was pissed. "You loyal fool." He almost hit him, but Blake stepped in to calm the situation. He ordered Dave to wait outside and let him negate the conversation.

"So, that's why you know this much about the case?" Blake started as soon as Dave left the room.

"Yes, but that doesn't mean I was involved with Mr Cooper. I know they were up to something, but this." He said in disgust. "I've never anticipated something like this from them."

"How can you be sure that Mr Cooper is the one?"

"Because one day I saw Mr Cooper. It was late at night, and I was just passing outside his house. Then I saw a man leaving the house. It was suspicious, but I decided to stay at a distance from them."

"Who was the guy?"

"I don't know. I have never seen him before, but his car plate was of Pinewood."

Blake was silent for a bit. "Well, Gary, I easily understand your story or narrative, but I have a question?"

"What is it, sir?"

"Why didn't you tell the police?" He continued. "We could've saved a lot of lives and even yours because, trust me, I will put you in jail so dark, you won't remember what the light is?"

"But sir, I told you everything. Don't do me like this." Gary started crying, but no one gave a damn about his tears. "I didn't do anything?"

"Yes, you didn't, and that's why you should also be in jail." Blake stood and started moving towards the door. "And listen, if you try to connect with Mr Cooper and decide to run out of town, I will hunt you down. So don't act smart and just play casual until I find the people behind all this mess."

Blake got out, and Dave waited for him the whole time.

"Well, supposedly, Mr Cooper murdered Philip," Blake said as he came out of the office.

"You're right, detective, but we can't keep our eyes off him." He indicated towards Gary's cabin.

"But we can't stay here forever, detective. Don't you have anyone on the backup who can monitor him?"

"Dave, this investigation is over in the eyes of the media and public. We can't make any noise because everyone in this case will be alerted. I need someone unofficial. Talk to your friends; maybe they can help us."

"Detective, I don't know if they are even willing to see my face."

Blake moved towards Dave and put his arm on his shoulder. "They won't, but just talk to them. Don't give them any major details; you'll be fine."

Dave understood the assignment and decided to call his friends from Pinewood. It was time to bury the past and make amends with one another.

XX
Making Amends

Dave tried calling Simon, but he didn't pick up his phone. He also tried reaching Elliot, but he was busy. It was clear that day that the two of them were ignoring him. He left a voice message for both of the guys, but it was not enough.

Now, there was no other option for Dave except to drive back to Pinewood and make amends with his friends.

Dave reached Elliot's place, but to his surprise, no one was there. He waited an hour, and it was almost evening. Then, a car arrived and stopped at the front gate. It was Elliot who was not happy to see the guest on his door.

"What the hell are you doing here?"

"Elliot, I want to talk to you?"

"Get out of my sight. I don't want to have a word with you."

"Listen, man, just listen," Dave said in frustration.

"What do you want now? Huh? Proving to find some dirt on me once again?"

"No, I need your help," Dave said in a low voice.

"Oh, just leave me alone. I don't want to help you."

"Elliot, you have to understand that it's a big point in the investigation."

"What the hell are you even talking about? Your detective caught the man already. I can't believe I bought drugs from a murderer." Elliot said traumatically. "So don't start with a new theory."

"Well, actually, I have a theory, or you can tell it a story."

Dave had no other option but to share the details of the case. It was naive or probably a mistake, but it was the only way to convince the man.

Elliot listened to the details very carefully, and by the end, his whole demeanour had changed. The move may have paid off.

Elliot was calm, and after a few moments of silence, he finally spoke out. "Alright, I can help you, but you have to be faster in your actions. I have work and don't have much time for all this."

"I know, and trust me, we'll be closing the case within a couple of days. We just need to find the guys, put them behind bars, and find Ella.

"I get it," Elliot said in an assured tone.

"Thanks, man. It means a lot, and please forgive me for the way I have been all the time. It was foolish, emotional, and stupid, so just try to understand."

"It's alright, man, and it's not as if I've been a saint all this time. I treated you like an enemy since you've been here and for a stupid thing. I apologise as well."

They both hugged, but then Dave realised that he was missing something. "Hey, do you have any idea about Simon? I am trying to reach him, but he's not picking up my phone."

"Yes, he went back to his home. He told me about your little altercation back at your apartment. He was really pissed at you and decided to leave town for the better."

"Alright, I'll catch up with him later. I have to finish this case first."

"Right, you should." Elliot started to walk towards his house. "Let me grab some stuff, and then we can leave for Silver Lake Town."

"Sure, I am waiting for you."

Elliot came back after a few minutes, carrying a small side bag." He decides to take his car since he'll have to come back as well.

The two drove separately to the hospital. Blake was waiting for them the whole time, and Aadi was also there. Apparently, the detective had called him to learn more about Mr Cooper and their current location. He got some useful information, which he can later use to track the family in case they get proper evidence against them.

Aadi and Elliot were finally on the same page when they decided to keep an eye on Gary Wise, who was still in the hospital. The four decided to communicate and update each other in case of any activity.

So all was set, and now the two investigators have to visit Mr Cooper. However, the detective needed to discuss something with Dave first.

"Dave, can you come here for a moment." The detective asked his subordinate to have a discussion.

"Yes, detective."

"Look, when you went back to Pinewood, I made some calls to track the car Gary Wise saw outside the Coopers' residence."

"Ok, did you find something?"

"Yes, and I don't know if this is just a coincidence, but the description of the car matched one specific person related to the case."

"Really, who?" Dave asked curiously.

"Jade."

"Are you serious?" Dave couldn't believe his ears.

"Yes, I am convinced that he, too, has his fair share in this entire series of events."

"Then maybe we should visit him first."

"That's what I am thinking."

"Alright, let's head to Jade's address."

Dave said energetically, but he was tired of moving back and forth between the two towns. However, he didn't have much choice. Plus, learning about Jade's association in the case is a big deal for both the guys.

Blake took control of the car and reached Jade's shop. It was a late night, so clearly, it was close, but Blake didn't want to take any chances. He then drove to his home. He knocked at the door for some time. Finally, Jade opened the door. The man was asleep, but as soon as he saw the investigators, all his sleep vanished.

"Detective, why are you here? Is everything alright?"

"Jade, I am sorry to disturb you at night, but there is a major update in the case, and I want to let you know about it. So, can we have a word or two?"

"Yes, sure. Come inside." Jade closed the door and blocked the cold breeze from the outside.

"Do you like some coffee? It's cold out there."

Blake looked at Dave. "Why not? Thanks."

Jade went to the kitchen, while Blake looked around the house. It was prominent compared to the other homes in Pinewood. Everything was so aesthetic and neat.

Jade had three big wooden almirahs that displayed books. He seemed like an avid reader or literary collector. He also had some artefacts on the top shelves which were unrecognisable to the two.

Dave was busy crafting an apology message to Simon. The two had their differences, but at the end of the day, both were doing what was best for them. Jade came with two cups of coffee. Blake was a bit suspicious and paranoid and decided to not drink the coffee. Meanwhile, Dave already had a couple of sips.

"You don't drink coffee?" Blake asked casually.

"It's midnight, and I don't want extra caffeine."

"Yes, it's dangerous for your brain, or so the study suggests."

"Well, I didn't hear about any such study, but maybe it's a possibility."

"It was more of an article, so you can't trust half the source. Maybe it's false, who knows?" Blake said to have a conversation.

Jade laughed a bit. "You're not wrong. So, what do you have on the case?"

"Well, we caught a guy, and you've probably heard about it."

"Yes, some officer called me in the evening and asked me about the man. And to be honest with you, I don't know him. Maybe he's a psychopath."

"Or maybe he's not the guy who did those murders." Dave intervened.

Jade was beginning to get a bit uncomfortable. "What do you mean? You caught him, right? So what's the catch?"

"Actually, we have some new leads in the case. A lead that takes us back to Mr Cooper. Do you know about him?"

"Yes, he was my customer in the shop; occasionally, he bought all kinds of unique stuff. But what does he have to do with the case?"

"His daughter, Ella, went missing almost a year back. And things were not the same in the town after her disappearance."

"Detective, pardon me, but I am not as sharp as you, so can you just elaborate on what you're up to?"

"We'll come to that, Jade, but first, I want to know why you helped him?"

"Help who?" He was getting a bit nervous. "Mr Cooper. You told me that you knew him. So you might be helping him in the crime."

"Oh, what rubbish?" Jade snapped and broke down. "How can you say something like this? You think I murdered my brother. What the hell is wrong with you?"

"Jade, calm down." Dave interfered because Jade was not the only one furious about the revelations.

"Look, Jade, we're just following the truth. And if you're in the way, it's better to speak up and tell us everything before it's too late. A genuine source saw your car outside the Cooper residence some months back. What's that about?"

Jade was speechless as if he had gone into trauma. After a few seconds, he was broken and started crying. He sank to his knees, and it was only a matter of time before he revealed his story. He finally looked at the investigators, took a deep breath and started to speak up.

"It was me, I kidnapped Ella."

Dave was expecting to hear this, but it was hard for him to fully articulate the sentence. He was lost, and when he came to his senses. He held Jade by the collar and was threatening him. He didn't even want to hear anything from the guy and just wanted to hurt him badly.

It was Blake who separated the two and once again asked Dave to leave for a few minutes. Blake understood that it was dangerous for him to keep Dave near Jade; however, he understood and, upon coming back, sat down quietly on the side.

XXI

Simple Complication

Jade struggled to even begin, as each word made him shiver to the spine. However, he knew that investigators would only leave him after he told them the truth.

"So it was probably last year. I was working at my shop, and things were going well business-wise. Mr Cooper was a regular customer at my shop. He always bought something, and from there, our friendship started. He was a decent and stand-up guy. However, one day, he came to my shop, and I could see that he was struggling. I had no idea what was going on? I should have never asked him."

He sighed with disappointment. "Anyway, I asked him about his situation, and he told me everything about Ella and her condition. They have tried everything, but there was no success. I was not able to see him in such poor condition, so I offered him my help."

"What kind of help?" Dave intervened.

"I know some medical professionals in the city. I asked to arrange a donor for Ella for a heart transplant. Upon hearing this, Mr Cooper was delighted. However, there was a catch to it."

"It was an illegal procedure," Blake said in a brutal tone.

"Yes, and it would have taken some time for the arrangements. Also, they might need a body for this purpose. Nevertheless, Mr Cooper gave me Ella's medical reports, which I sent to the city so that the doctors could find the ideal donor."

He drank some water from a cup on the table. "A few weeks passed and there was no update from the city. Mr Cooper came to me every day but left with disappointment. However, one day, the bell rang, and they had arranged a donor, but it would take around 4-5 months before the operation. I called Mr Cooper, and he was beyond joy. But when he came to me, he was sad and lost. I asked him what happened? He told me that Ella knew about our arrangement, and she was declining to take organs harvested after taking the life of some innocent person. She would rather die than live with that guilt. It broke Mr Cooper, and to be fair, I completely respected Ella's decision. But you know parents, and they can go beyond limits to save their children. Well, something similar happened with Mr Cooper. He had so many arguments with Ella, but she won't budge. And one day, he decided to go against her daughter's will."

"He asked you to kidnap Ella!" Dave said with a straight and tense face.

"You could say it's more of an assistance. So Mr Cooper came to me and told me that Ella was planning to leave Pinewood and travel around the world before she died. So, now the only way to stop her was to kidnap her and take her to the city for operation. At first, I thought that it was insanity, but then I looked at Mr Cooper, and I couldn't refuse—he might kill himself if something happened to Ella. So, we made a plan to kidnap Ella and keep her safe till the date of the operation came. And it worked; on the eve of the party, when everyone left, Mr Cooper sedated her and called me. I had already made arrangements on my brother's farm—there was a room that was locked for years. Ella would be safe there, and no one would ever notice."

"But someone did," Blake sneered at the guy. "So, what happened next?"

"Well, there were not many issues in the first few months, but with time, Mr Cooper grew impatient, and he was angry all the time. He snapped at me for the delay with the doctors in the city. At the same time, Ella's health was deteriorating, but there was nothing I could have done."

"So you killed her?" Dave said angrily.

"No, I didn't kill her."

"Detective, he's lying."

"Dave, just calm yourself." He looked at Jade. "What about your brother? Did he know about the mess that you created behind his back?"

"No, he had no idea, and I tried to keep it that way."

"So why did you kill him?"

"Detective! I didn't murder him. Even that is a different story. I was not in town, and upon hearing the news, I was devastated. I might have kidnapped Ella, but it was for her safety."

Blake horrifyingly punched the guy. "Then where is she? Huh? What happened to her and your brother?"

"Sir, I told you everything already. I didn't know I was away, and when I heard the news, my world turned upside down. She was gone from her room, and my brother was dead. That's all I know. Please trust me; I am telling you the truth."

Blake stood up. "Where is Mr Cooper?" He asked gently. "Where is she?" And then he shouted.

"I don't know. I haven't talked with him in so long. After the incident, he asked me to cut ties so that I was safe. That's all I know."

"Alright." He took a deep breath and started typing on his phone. "The police will be here in half an hour. You're arrested for kidnapping the missing girl. You can call a lawyer or whatever. I don't care, but let me tell you one thing before I go, your act of false bravery cost two people their lives. So, think about that before doing your so-called noble act."

The two waited for the police to arrive. Jade was taken into custody, and now the investigators have to find the Cooper family. Luckily, Aadi had already tracked them and sent the address to Blake.

They were in the nearby city, and now the two had to bring them in. Without wasting any time, the two started their journey to the city. It was very far, so they had to be quick in their action. Upon reaching the city, they went to the given address.

It was a posh society and very peaceful. The investigators reached the apartment, and when the door opened, Mr Cooper was astonished to see the two guys at that hour of the day.

He immediately understood their reason to be there, and without wasting a second, he asked to say some things to his wife. The door was still open. He went inside, and the two waited just out of respect for the man. He came back and closed the door before. "Let's go outside. I guess you've finally found your man."

The three of them went to a small bench in a small park just outside the seven-story building. The investigators had only one question: 'Why?'

All of them sat, and Mr Cooper started to explain everything. "So, I guess you've already talked with Jade."

"Yes, sir, we just want to know your end of the story."

"Alright, but let Jade go; he had no idea about anything."

"Oh, shut up!" Dave was impatient. "Just answer your questions before I snap at a senior."

"I am sorry, Dave. I know the first time I saw you coming back from the city that someday you'll find me and look, here I am before your eyes." He looked at Blake. "I have killed Philip; he was a good man but at the wrong place."

"What exactly happened?"

"Well, I suppose you know that Jade was out of town. So, it was up to me to take care of Ella. She was in a remote place on the farm, but I don't know how, but Philip found her. He was trying to help her and set her free. He was successful, but I can't let that happen. I reached the place exactly at the time and saw the two on the door. I tried my best to explain, but he won't listen. He came between Ella and me, and she ran. I tried to chase her, but he stopped. The confrontation went to the ground, and I got hold of a big rock, and I hit him. I didn't have any idea that he would die. I will get to know about that later. I was so worried, plus there was a man on the scene."

"You mean Rick?"

"Yes, he was there, and when I saw Philip. I ran from there, but I was not sure if he saw my face. After all this, it was only me who had to work alone and erase everything on the case."

"What about Ella?" Dave asked with curiosity. "Where is she?"

There were tears in Mr Cooper's eyes. "That was the last time I saw her, and I guess it was meant to be that way."

"Stop with nonsense, and just tell me where did she go?"

"Dave, I am sorry, but I don't know. She didn't have much time to live, and considering her health, I don't know if she's even alive."

"You don't know that," Dave shouted.

"If she was alive and wanted me behind bars, she would have already done it."

Mr Cooper had a point. Blake saw the tensions between the two, so he acted to keep things moderate. He tried to gain the attention of Mr Cooper once again, who was busy shedding tears.

"What about the car?"

"I stole it so that no one can recognise my car. I used it to frighten Rick and eliminate him when he was under your custody. I had to just keep my eye on Dave because I knew he was not an official. When I had no use for the car, I ditched it."

"Well, you were almost successful in framing that thief. How do you know about him?"

"It was Sunday in Silver Lake Town, and I was coming from somewhere. Then I saw that drug dealer handing drugs to some kids in the alley, on the side of the street. I didn't know anything about him, but he seemed to be the exact guy I could use to ditch the car. I could have done this by myself, but that would have been a waste of parts. So, I decided to leave the car in front of his place. He was foolish and greedy to take the bait, and my job was done. I had already removed most of the fingerprints using chemicals, so the forensics couldn't catch me. Also, I didn't have my fingerprints in the police database, which makes me a complete stranger in your eyes."

Blake laughed. "Well, here we are, so I guess you failed big time."

"I knew it was only a matter of time. I tried everything to get out of Pinewood and Silver Lake Town, but I guess your vices will always follow you, no matter the location."

"Seems like it." Blake sighed and looked at Dave, who was ready to throw some punches. "Why did you kill Rick? He didn't have any idea about you. First, you threatened him, and then you shot him dead. Why is that?"

"As I said before, I didn't know much about him. After I threatened him, he was gone, and I was perturbed. What if he was in police custody? But later, I came to know that you guys were keeping him away. I know that Dave was helping you in the investigation. So, I kept an eye on him, and fortunately, he led me to Rick and rest, you know already."

"You're a murderer, Mr Cooper, and a sick human being," Dave said as he felt somewhat responsible for having a man killed.

"So, you don't know where Ella is?" Blake intervened before instigating the matter.

"No, sir, you have to trust me. She's my daughter; I want to see her more than anyone else in this world. I tried searching for her everywhere, but she was gone. I guess I failed not only as a parent but as a human being."

"Don't worry, Mr Cooper, you will have plenty of time to reflect on that after your prosecution." Dave looked at the balcony and saw Mrs Cooper keeping an eye on them. "If you want to say something to her, I won't stop you. You can have your moment with her."

"No, I am ok, she'll be fine."

"Alright, you're coming with us to Pinewood as we hand you over to the police."

"Alright, Detective." He looked at Dave. "You are a good guy, Dave. I wish things would have been different."

Dave didn't even bother to make eye contact. He was still thinking about Ella, but now he had reached the end of the road, and clearly, there was nowhere he could've gone from there.

XXII

A Faded Sight

Three months passed after Mr Cooper was charged with murdering two innocent people and kidnapping his own daughter. Jade and Gary were also behind bars for helping with the criminal acts. Rob was free and back on the streets, but he was working at a local restaurant this time and not selling drugs.

After everything happened, he wanted to leave his drug life behind and start from scratch. Mrs Cooper was in trauma after learning about her husband, and her wounds might never heal.

Elliot was in Pinewood studying, dedicated to clearing his coming exams. Meanwhile, Detective Blake went on a much-needed vacation. He received some sort of funding from the police department, and he decided to take some time off. He wanted to reflect on life and accept what was in store for him in the future.

Dave went back to the city and finally got a job. He explained everything to his family, and even though his parents were mad at him initially, they were relieved to know he was safe and returning to everyday life.

Dave returned to the city after spending a few days with the family. He had his own place, and everything was normal—he and Simon were friends again, and he was enjoying his time at work. However, he was still thinking about Ella and one day, he received a call from Ivan, his cousin. He wanted Dave to come to his place as soon as possible. Dave reached Ivan's apartment, who was cleaning the place.

"Here, I was cleaning the house and found a letter with your name on it." He handed the letter to his brother. "I am sorry. I now remember that it was in front of my door around four months back. I thought to give it when you'd come back, but you didn't, and I forgot about this until today when I stumbled upon it."

"No problem. It's just a letter. I'll read it." Dave replied with a smile.

"Yeah sure, you can go inside, that room is clean."

"Thanks."

Dave took it and went inside to read it. He sat on a couch and opened it. The letter was from Ella, and Dave couldn't believe his eyes. He was hesitant to read it, but he was ready after a couple of deep breaths. It started:

"Hi Dave, if you're reading this, I am most likely dead. I guess you already know about my health, but that's not why I am writing to you. I want to thank you for being a part of my life. I didn't expect anyone to ever fight for me except you, and you did. I am wrong for ditching our relationship last year, but I was broken inside, and my emotions got the better of me. But that's the past, and I want you to focus on the present. You're a decent man; maybe now it's time to look at the future. You have a whole life ahead, and I wish I could be part of it, but that's not how destiny works! I wish you the best and am sorry I couldn't have a final conversation with you, but remember, whenever you're on a dark night, I'll be with you through a faded sight.

Love,
Ella."